FITTING IN

A BIMBO TRANSFORMATION NOVEL

SADIE THATCHER

"Why won't you come out right?" Kristen mumbled to herself in anger. She sat in her cubicle, staring at her computer screen. The numbers were not adding up right. There was an error someplace, probably just a typo, but she needed to find it before she could submit her final report for the quarter. She was looking forward to going home for a well deserved break.

The holidays had just ended and Kristen had barely been able to keep up with her job and her social commitments. Actually, that was not entirely true. Her social commitments were not that time consuming. She had few friends. However, as a natural introvert, Kristen needed a lot of time to get herself ready for anything much more than lunch or drinks with a small group of friends.

The company New Year's Eve party had taken a lot out of Kristen. She appreciated the change from her old job when such a large emphasis was placed on Christmas and an annual Christmas party. Not that Kristen did not celebrate Christmas. She did. It was just that a company Christmas party, in her opinion, seemed to give her Christmas overload.

And spreading out the events she felt the need to attend with one a week after the big holiday made things easier.

Not that much easier, however. Kristen needed lots of time to psyche herself up for this year's party. The whole thing was fun, but definitely mentally draining. It did not help that Kristen felt completely underdressed. She had no idea that people went all out with fancy dresses and tuxedos at the event. She stuck out like a sore thumb wearing her black slacks and blue sweater. She had thought it was perfect until she showed up to see some of the women in gowns.

Kristen almost went home right then, knowing this scene was not for her. She felt frustrated, because no dress code had been mentioned in her invitation. She had not even needed to bring any food to share with her. The whole event had been catered. Maybe that should have been a signal that she needed to dress up more.

The sensory and social overload left Kristen exhausted all weekend. That exhaustion carried over into her first week of the new year. The company's financial numbers had finally been collected and it was Kristen's job to put together the end of year report. Numbers had always come easy for her, but these numbers were causing nothing but difficulty. For whatever reason, they were not adding up as they should.

"Excuse me," came a male voice, surprising Kristen.

She looked up from her computer to see a man she never expected to see standing in the entrance to her small cubicle. Her mouth fell open, her tongue almost falling out of her mouth.

The man was Blake Worthington, the company Vice President of Accounting and Finance. He was her boss' boss' boss' boss' boss, or something like that. The gap between him and her was so big she never had any expectation to ever meet him, let alone have him suddenly standing at the entrance to her cubicle. There were so many levels of bureaucracy in between them that she did not even think they were supposed to talk to each other.

"You're Kristen Peterson, right?" he asked.

"Um, I mean, yes, Mr. Worthington," Kristen answered, finally getting herself together and pushing down her sudden fear and trepidation. It seemed unlikely that the Vice President of her division would be the one to fire her. There had to be another reason for his seeking her out.

"Please, call me Blake," he said with a kind smile. "I've never liked people calling me by my last name. It makes me sound like my father and I don't want anything to do with that man."

"Um, okay." Kristen's nervousness was rising again. "What can I do for you, Blake?"

"This is awkward," Blake answered. "I'm probably not supposed to do this during work hours, if at all, but I have a confession to make. You see, I saw you at the party last week and—"

"I'm terribly sorry about my appearance at the party," Kristen jumped in. "Had I known the kind of party it was, I would have dressed up more or not come at all. I should have just left when I saw all the other women wearing fancy dresses."

"Oh," Blake said, slightly flummoxed by Kristen's defense of herself. "I didn't mean that at all. I was going to say that I saw you and I was wondering if you would like to get coffee sometime?"

Kristen stared up into Blake's eyes, a look of confusion on her face. His words made no sense. This was not the sort of thing that ever happened to her. The only people who ever asked Kristen out were losers and perverts. Or at least that was the bulk of her experience. She had never considered herself a magnet for men. Her shyness usually left her with whatever was leftover after the prettier women picked over the selection.

"You're asking me out on a date?" Kristen finally asked, piecing it all together and accepting that this was actually happening. However, she still needed to be sure.

"Just a coffee date," Blake answered. "Nothing too serious. We hardly know each other. But you intrigue me and I am interested in getting to know you better."

"Wow," Kristen said. "I don't know what to say."

"Before you make a decision, I want you to know that your job with the company is completely unrelated to my request. If you turn me down, there will be no consequences other than me not buying you a cup of coffee. Nor will accepting my offer help you get a promotion. This is purely social and outside the scope of your job. There might be other disclaimers I should make, but I can't think of them right now. Suffice it to say, any impropriety on my part in me asking you is wholly on me and I will not hold anything against you if you turn me down. I don't play office politics like that."

As Kristen sat there, posed with the great question of whether she wanted to accept a coffee date with the Vice President in charge of her division, she also had to come to terms with exactly who was asking. Blake Worthington was one of six Vice Presidents of the company. He was also one of what was sometimes referred to as the Big Three. He, along with Darren Carver and Mike Shockley, were smart, young, and seemingly full of ambition. There were rumors within the company that they were being fast tracked for future C-suite roles.

Blake was probably the most handsome of the trio, although definitely in a J. Crew kind of way. He looked every bit the young and hot executive with almost roguish good looks and a certain aloofness to his style that made him hard to pin down. He showed up to work everyday wearing perfectly stylish and tailored suits. Beyond that, Kristen never saw him, however, he was rumored to be a big basketball fan and would play at the gym on his way into work at least once a week.

The Big Three were also known for the company they kept. The three entered the company as friends and their friendship had only strengthened. But it was more than that. It was the women who always seemed to be in their orbit that left Kristen scratching her head as to why Blake would approach her. Of all the women in the company, she should not have been high on his list. She was not glamorous. She was not sexy. She was just plain. And with his money, Blake could attract any kind of woman he wanted. So that left the big question. Why her?

However, Kristen knew there was only one way to truly understand why Blake had approached her. She could ask now, before accepting the date, but she did not really have time for that. She needed to finish this report. Then she could take a few days off, read a good book or two, and return to the office next week fully refreshed. Blake was interrupting her plans.

"Okay, I accept," Kristen finally said. She was curious about why Blake had asked her and she intended to find out. But that line of questioning would need to wait until they were outside the office.

"Fantastic," Blake said. He seemed genuinely excited. "I'll have my secretary… You know what, it's probably best to leave me secretary out of it. I'll text you tonight and we can decide on a time and place. How does that sound?"

"Perfect," Kristen said as she started to write out her phone number on a sticky note.

"Thanks," Blake said as she handed him the note. "I probably could have looked it up, but this way no one needs to ask any questions."

"Right," Kristen agreed, wondering if she had just made a big mistake. Blake Worthington asking her out was definitely not on her bingo card for the new year.

"I'll let you get back to work. Have a nice day. I'll text you later."

Blake was gone before Kristen had a chance to say anything. Then again, she did not know what she should say. The whole thing had left her confused.

2

"Hi, Kristen," came an unexpected voice as Kristen sat in the cafeteria eating her lunch. She had a series of spreadsheet printouts in front of her, as she continued to go over the data for her report.

Kristen looked up to find two women she expected to talk to her standing over her, each holding a tray of food.

"Can we join you?" the other woman asked.

"Um, sure," Kristen said, confused. The past two days had been weirder and weirder. First Blake Worthington asked her out on a coffee date and now the two hottest women at the company, secretaries for the Vice Presidents, had decided to join her for lunch.

The two women carefully sat across from Kristen. They took their time, wiping down the bench seat with napkins before they risked sitting on it in their short skirts.

"I'm Abbi," the redhead said, introducing herself.

"And I'm Nikki," said the brunette.

"And we hear you've got a date with Blake," Abbi said.

"So much for keeping that discreet," Kristen said. She had texted back and forth with Blake the night before, arranging for a Saturday coffee date at a local coffee shop. Kristen had chosen the place, partly because she knew what they offered. But she also had a good idea that no one at the shop would recognize either of them. There would be no reports to HR about her seeing a company VP outside of work. What they were doing was not prohibited, but it was frowned upon, at least at the levels Kristen worked at. It could be different in the upper echelons of the company. Kristen had no way of knowing that.

"And how did you hear that?" she asked, wanting to know where the leak happened. The date was supposed to be off the books and a secret.

"Blake told Darren and Mike and they told us," Nikki answered. "They want us to make sure you look your best for your date."

"And what business is it of yours or theirs how I look on my date?" Kristen asked icily. Her two lunchtime companions were not the type of women she usually associated herself with. They seemed far more interested in their appearances than in their work. It was little wonder that they were secretaries when she was an accountant. As far as Kristen knew, Abbi and Nikki had not needed any actual qualifications before getting hired, outside of being hot and probably a willingness to put out.

"We like Blake and we want what's best for him," Abbi said. "And believe it or not, we like you and we want you to be happy. Blake is a good guy and if you're the right woman for him, then we're happy."

"Look, you don't have to like us," Nikki added. "We just thought you might like a few pointers to help get ready for your date. That's all."

Kristen closed her eyes and took a deep breath. When she opened them again, she spoke, "I'm sorry. I'm just really stressed out right now. I've got to finish this report so I can take a few days off and recharge. It's been a crazy last couple weeks with it being the end of the quarter and with the holidays and everything. I just need a break."

Both women smiled. "We know just the thing to help," Abbi said as she started digging around in her clutch purse. It was not very big, but it was bulging with everything Abbi had stuck inside it. She kept an array of makeup products at her desk to make sure she always looked her best, but there were some items, like lipstick, she kept in her purse. She wore a different shade everyday, at least every day of the week, so she carried that, along with a few other important items, in her purse.

"There's this salon," Nikki explained while Abbi continued to rummage through her purse. "It's called Woman Magic. It's the best salon ever. It's like they really perform magic there. I go at least once a month."

"Here we go," Abbi said as she pulled out a card from her purse. She put it on the table and slid it across to Kristen. "Set up an appointment for Friday. Or even better yet, for Saturday morning. I guarantee you'll both look great and feel great for your date."

Kristen picked up the offered card and looked at it more closely. "Woman Magic," she read. "Powered by B Enterprises. I've never heard of this place or this B Enterprises before."

"It's very exclusive," Nikki said. "They only take on new clients that have been recommended by a current client. There's a code on the back of the card that will get you an appointment."

"Trust us," Abbi said. "This place is a life changer. You won't regret it."

"I suppose I could use a bit of a style upgrade," Kristen mused as she held a few strands of her shoulder length coppery blonde hair in front of her face. "I guess I should thank you for your advice."

"You and Blake just have a nice time and that will be thanks enough," Nikki said.

"We've got to get back to our desks," Abbi added. "Darren and Mike like us to be nearby at the end of their lunch hours."

"We'll talk next week," Nikki said. "Have fun this weekend."

"Thanks," Kristen said as she absentmindedly spun the card around in her fingers. "I'll talk to you later."

3

It had taken Kristen nearly half an hour to recover from her lunchtime visit from Abbi and Nikki. They had this weird effect on her that made it hard to concentrate after talking to them. However, she was thankful for the advice they had provided. Despite their seemingly high maintenance personalities clashing with Kristen's down to earth style, she appreciated how they had sought her out, wanting to help.

And this was definitely one of those situations where Kristen was not above asking for help. None of her rare dates ever seemed to go anywhere. She simply had never attracted a guy who she felt comfortable with. Not that Blake was any better in terms of her feeling comfortable with him. However, the difference between Blake and the other guys she had recently gone on dates with was one of station. If Kristen was honest with herself, she had always dated below her standing. The men she had gone out with had few prospects for themselves, both personally and financially. Blake, on the other hand, was the opposite. He seemed so far beyond her that she seriously questioned whether a relationship with him could work.

But that was why Kristen found herself at Magic Woman Saturday morning, only a few hours before her date with Blake. She had finally finished her end of quarter report and had taken the previous few days off from work. In that time she had finished two books she had been meaning to read and had completely recovered from the combination of the New Year's Eve party and the mad dash to get the numbers figured out for her report.

As soon as Kristen walked into Magic Woman, she felt as if she was having a meeting with Abbi and Nikki again. They were the glamorous and sexy women that the Big Three had always gone for and the women who worked at Magic Woman were similar.

"Hi, you must be Kristen," the woman at the front desk said with a big smile when Kristen approached.

"Um, yeah, that's me," Kristen replied, feeling more self-conscious than ever. She was beginning to regret wearing a sweatshirt and loose jeans to her appointment. The woman behind the desk was decked out in a tight red dress that looked more like it belonged on the dance floor of a nightclub than in the lobby of a salon. The woman's breasts seemed to bulge out of the top of the dress, enhancing her already impressive cleavage. Kristen could not see the woman's lower half, but she could guess that the dress revealed her legs just as much as it did her breasts.

"I'm Penny. We spoke on the phone earlier this week. I have you down for the Basic Beauty Lift. Is that still what you are looking for?"

"Yeah, I think so," Kristen said. "I don't know that I'm ready for anything more than that. And I probably don't have time either. You see, I've got a coffee date later today. I don't want to be late for that."

"I'll let your stylist know about that," Penny said. "Why don't you have a seat and Gabby will be out in a moment for you?"

Kristen took a seat and watched as Penny got up and walked through the door into the back of the salon. Unlike most salons, Magic Woman seemed to conduct the bulk of its business outside the view from the street. It made Kristen wonder why until she remembered the code on the back of the card she had needed to make her appointment. Apparently this was a situation where exclusivity was a major selling factor. The price she had been quoted on the phone was certainly more than she would normally spend when getting her hair done, but considering who she was about to go on a date with, she figured such an expense would be worth it. It would certainly demonstrate her seriousness, assuming Blake even noticed. Men were sometimes less than observant about such matters.

Kristen did note that Penny's dress was as short as she had figured it might be. Penny needed to tug it down when she got up, but that only brought the hem down to the top of her thighs. The shoes were another matter and something Kristen had not fully anticipated. The heel on her shoes had to be at least six inches high. Then again, with the thick platform sole, the angle on her feet was not as extreme. It still forced Penny to totter instead of walk properly.

When the door opened next, Kristen watched as Penny came out followed by a woman who must have been Gabby. If Penny looked like she was headed to a nightclub, Gabby looked like she had just gotten home from one. Her blonde hair looked a little wild, as if she had spent all night dancing. Her dress was similar to Penny's, but it was black and featured a series of rips across her midriff. Her makeup gave her a roguish appearance, which contributed to the idea that she might have been out all night.

"Kristen, I'm Gabby," the woman said, confirming her identity. "If you'll come back with me, we can get started."

"Um sure," Kristen said, pushing herself to her feet and following Gabby with a slow shuffle. "It looks like you had a long night."

"Oh, um, well, yeah, I guess," Gabby answered. "My hours are all screwed up. But I usually go clubbing before I start work in the morning. I've got to focus on what I enjoy most. But don't worry, you're in good hands. Although I usually have a few more minutes to get myself put together before my shift. It's not often we have clients quite this early."

"I've got a date to get ready for," Kristen explained. "That's the reason for my early appointment. I doubt it will happen again."

Gabby laughed. "That's quite all right. No worries. This will be our booth for the day."

Gabby led Penny into a stall that featured all the usual salon accommodations. The counter was even covered in the usual array of hair and makeup products.

Kristen automatically took a seat.

"Penny tells me you have chosen the Basic Beauty Lift package," Gabby said as she moved several products around the counter, getting everything just how she wanted it. "That's a good starting place, I think. Especially for you, what with your upcoming date and all. I would try and upsell you, but you probably don't have time unless it's a late date."

"It's not," Kristen said. "It's just coffee."

"Ah, the coffee date," Gabby said with a chuckle. "I haven't been on one of those in ages. I kind of miss those."

Kristen decided not to ask about the kinds of dates Gabby went on most of the time, assuming she went on dates at all. Given what Gabby had already admitted, Kristen had the impression that her stylist was more into the hookup culture of clubbing than in forming lasting romantic relationships.

Kristen definitely fell into the latter category, although she had a hard time seeing anything romantic coming out of her coffee date with Blake. He just seemed like too unlikely of a partner in her eyes.

"Just to go over what you have in store for you," Gabby continued, however, she had switched over to business and became more serious. "Your chosen package comes with hair and makeup. There are a few other little bonuses I can explain if you want or I can just get to work."

"Let's just get to work," Kristen replied. "I don't have a mind to hold onto all those details."

"Understandable," Gabby said. "But one last question. How would you feel about going a bit lighter with your hair? I think it could look really good."

Kristen shrugged her shoulders. She had never been a big fan of her hair, but she had never cared enough to change it. This seemed like a good enough time to try something different. Maybe she would like it. Maybe Blake would too. "Sure, why not. Go for it."

"Excellent. When we're done here, you'll almost feel like a whole new person."

4

Kristen arrived at the coffee shop feeling as if her whole morning had been a blur. And truth be told, it had been a blur. After giving Gabby the go ahead to lighten her hair, she remembered little of her actual appointment. Although Kristen had to admit Gabby did good work.

After returning home from Magic Woman, Kristen had spent almost half an hour just staring at her reflection in the mirror. She had the hardest time seeing her reflection as herself. It was uncanny and a little unnerving, assuming one ignored how good she now looked.

First and foremost, it was impossible to ignore her hair. Her once thin and boring hair, that bordered just barely on the blonde side of the blonde-brunette divide, was now fully blonde, and a very light blonde at that. What was more, it had somehow gained in both volume and length since she woke up that morning. How Gabby had pulled it off, she had no idea, but she knew there were no extensions involved.

But it was not just her hair that left Kristen staring. Her face looked different too. Some of that was makeup to be sure, but not everything could be explained away by clever use of makeup. Both Kristen's nose and cheekbones looked different. The former looked thinner and almost more doll-like and the latter looked higher and more regal. Combined all together, she could almost think she was a different person.

It also quickly became apparent that Kristen's original date outfit was simply not going to cut it. Her hair and makeup demanded a slightly more upscale look than what she had originally planned, which had essentially been a variation of the same outfit she had worn to the New Year's Eve party. She replaced the sweater from that night with a pink one. It was a minor change, but it seemed to suit her hair and makeup.

The black slacks and black flats were more difficult to replace. Kristen had to dig into the back of her closet to find the black pencil skirt. She also had to dig around the back to find the heels she wore with them. At least she already had the black hose, although she hoped Blake did not have x-ray vision that could see the run up the back that her skirt thankfully covered.

"I'm going shopping soon," Kristen told herself as she walked into the coffee shop. She paused just inside the door, scanning the shop to see if Blake had arrived yet. He had not. Kristen had planned for this. She wanted to arrive first, partly as a test to see how Blake treated the baristas and anyone else he might encounter. She also did not want to receive any criticism for her order. Kristen actually hated the taste of coffee, thus making her coffee date a bit laughable. But hot chocolate looked enough like some of the coffee drinks that she could pass it off as coffee without anyone bothering her.

Kristen was quick to order. She then selected a booth off to the side of the shop. From where she sat, she could watch both the door and the counter, giving her a perfect vantage point to make sure Blake was really the nice guy that he at least pretended to be.

Just as Kristen's drink was delivered to her, she spotted Blake walking by the front window. He stopped in front of the door for a moment and looked up, as if he was making sure that this was indeed the place they were meeting. Satisfied that it was, he opened the door and walked in.

Kristen watched as he scanned the room. A part of her worried he might not recognize her with her newly colored hair. She had to admit that he looked good. His coffee date outfit turned out to be a green crew neck shirt beneath a sport coat, a pair of jeans, and running shoes. He was dressed up enough for a date, but also casual enough to make it clear this was just coffee.

As soon as Blake spotted Kristen, his eyes lit up. He walked over and gracefully slid into the booth across from her.

"Hi," he said, somewhat awkwardly.

"Hi, yourself," Kristen said, suddenly feeling much better about the whole event. Maybe Blake was just another regular guy who just happened to be really good at a high paying job that afforded him luxuries that Kristen was unaccustomed to.

"I see you already got a drink," Blake said. "I was figuring I would pay, since it was me who asked you out."

"It's just coffee," Kristen countered, smiling.

"Or hot chocolate in your case," Blake said. "Don't worry your secret is safe with me."

Kristen's face and neck turned red as she blushed in embarrassment. She had hoped not to avoid that observation.

"Do you mind if I go up to the counter and order?" Blake asked.

"Go right ahead."

As Blake slid out of the booth and pushed himself back to his feet, Kristen began to wonder if it had been worth getting her hair done for the date. Blake had not seemed to notice it. That made him a typical man, she supposed.

However, Blake paused after rising to his feet. He leaned over and whispered in Kristen's ear, "By the way, I like the hair. It looks good on you."

Kristen bit her lip as Blake walked up to the counter and made his order. The way the compliment had come, she was left in shock. She even almost forgot that she wanted to watch Blake's interaction with the baristas up at the counter. It was in moments like those that people often showed their true colors. A positive interaction would go a long way to show that Blake was genuinely good and that money had not corrupted him.

It was only a minute later that Blake had returned to his spot across from Kristen. She had not seen anything that warned her off of continuing the date. Blake seemed to have chatted happily with the people working behind the counter and their smiles got bigger when he placed a couple bills in the tip jar. Not that Kristen could see the denomination of the bills, but he had clearly tipped well on a relatively small purchase. That was a bonus point in her eyes.

"I want to lay out a couple ground rules before we start," Blake said as she got comfortable. "When we're here together, we don't talk about work. I'm sure you knew enough about me when I'm at work that we don't need to waste time on that. And to be honest, if I wanted to know what kind of employee you are, I could just look up your personnel record. I want to get to know you and hopefully you are interested in getting to know me."

"I think that makes sense," Kristen said.

"So, what have you been up to the past couple days?" Blake asked. "Other than getting your hair done, that is."

Kristen smiled. That was an easy question to get things started with. And in some ways, it was actually nice not having to talk about work. They could talk about the things they were interested in outside of work. That made for much more interesting conversations.

As for answering Blake's question, Kristen happily launched into stories about her two most recent read books. One was a biography of Theodore Roosevelt and the other was a novel featuring an autistic young man making his way in the world. And if Blake thought either book sounded boring, he certainly did not show it. He listened intently and even asked a few follow-up questions, demonstrating his interest and breadth of knowledge of history and the lives lived by people with autism. Kristen was impressed.

"What about you?" Kristen asked after she had finished describing what she had been doing with her days off of work. "How do you like to spend your free time?"

"I've got my basketball," Blake explained. "But you probably already knew that. It's no secret when I walk into the building with my gym bag and ball. Oops, I mentioned work. I broke my own rule. Okay, what else do I like to do."

Blake then launched into various projects and events he was involved in. Kristen was impressed with how many charities Blake seemed to actively participate in. He did not just cut checks and leave them be. He was active in several of them, helping to organize events or acting as a drum beat to encourage his peers to donate time and money.

As Kristen sat there, conversing with Blake, she found herself really enjoying his company. He seemed like a great guy and she definitely found him attractive. He was fit and smart. Other than his job making him tons of money, she began to wonder if she had truly been dating the wrong people all her life. Yes, there had been little success in her dating life up until this point, but there might have been a reason for that. Maybe she simply had not taken care to make herself available to the kind of men she actually wanted to be with.

Blake and Kristen sat there talking for over two hours. It was the longest date Kristen had experienced in years. Previous dates had rarely extended past the hour mark. They had been that bad. But this was going swimmingly and for the first time in who knew how long, she was actually anticipating a second date.

"Listen, Kristen," Blake said as things started to wind down. The coffee shop was set to close soon too. "I'd like to see you again. I'm going out of town on business next week, but when I get back, I'd like to take you out to dinner. This time I'm buying."

Kristen looked into her empty mug for a moment. She had been idly playing with it ever since she had finished it, giving her something to do with her hands. She smiled. "Yes, I'd like that," she said, looking up and meeting Blake's warm green eyes.

"Fantastic," Blake said. "We can figure out a night that works well via text."

Both Kristen and Blake slid out of the booth in unison and stood up. There was a moment of awkwardness as they decided how they wanted to part company.

"It was nice to do this," Kristen said, breaking the silence as she reached in for a hug.

"If you don't mind, a hug doesn't demonstrate how I feel," Blake said. "Would you mind if I kiss you?"

Kristen's mind flashed back to a memory in college. It was her freshman year and there was a speaker that came to campus at the start of the year and the big message was to ask to kiss before actually going in for the kiss. Kristen and everyone she knew laughed it off at the time, but she had to admit the first date kisses she had experienced were usually not as welcome as her dates assumed they were. Blake was the first man to ask her.

"I think I'd like that," Kristen said.

And just like that, Blake's lips were on hers and she loved it. This was not a kiss with lots of tongue, it was not the kind that led to making out, it was not a hot and passionate kiss. This was a kiss that made a promise. It promised more. And it was a promise that made Kristen feel like she could not wait another week or more before she felt Blake's lips against hers again.

5

"So, how was it?" Abbi asked as she and Nikki joined Kristen at lunch the following Monday. Blake was off on his business trip, meaning Kristen could not be tempted to try and move up their next date. And she would have been tempted if the laws of physics allowed her to be in two places at once or to travel at faster than the speed of light. Since neither was possible, she was stuck wishing, hoping, and fantasizing.

And talking to Abbi and Nikki. They had inserted themselves into Kristen's life and she was not sure how she felt about that. The truth was, she did not have many friends at work. She was new enough that she had not managed to meet many people and she was shy enough that she had not sought anyone out. She had also been plain enough that others had not sought her out.

That was until Blake had asked her out. Kristen was still not sure what he saw in her. She was just a boring woman who worked with numbers all day. Her idea of a fun weekend was curling up on the couch under a warm blanket and reading a book while sipping on a big mug of hot chocolate.

"It was…" Kristen said, trailing off with a smile on her face. "It was nice."

"Nice?" Nikki said in disbelief. "That's all you can say about it? It was nice?"

"What?" Kristen countered. "What's wrong with nice? It's not like I went home with him. It was just a coffee date. But we're going to get dinner when he gets back from his trip."

"Nothing is wrong with nice," Abbi said as she shot a side glance at Nikki that seemed to mean shut up. "But it must be hard waiting for a second date. Blakes business trips often get extended."

"I didn't know that," Kristen said, suddenly depressed that her next time seeing Blake would be even later than she had anticipated.

"It happens to all the VPs," Nikki said with a shrug. "They always underestimate how much time it will take to negotiate new contracts or complete reorganizations. If they would only ask us, their secretaries, it might be easier. Abbi usually wins the travel pool. She's really good with her predictions."

"When do you think Blake will return?" Kristen asked, hopeful it would not be too long. She had hoped to see him again over the upcoming weekend, but that was less promising now.

"Probably late Monday," Abbi said confidently. "Tuesday at the latest."

"Oh," Kristen said. "I guess that's not so bad."

"Enough about all that travel," Nikki said, seemingly bored with the direction the conversation had taken. "How do you like your hair? I think it looks fab."

"You really like it?" Kristen asked. A giddiness bubbled up inside of her from the compliment. She had never received a compliment like that from a woman before. Yes, it had felt good to hear Blake compliment her hair during the date, but this was different. This was a compliment from someone who clearly already knew something about style and fashion. Nikki and Abbi always looked fantastic.

"Girl," Abbi said. "You've got sexy hair now. I bet Blake loved it."

Kristen blushed at the further compliment. "He did mention it."

"I knew it," Abbi said. "Blake has always been a sucker for blondes."

"But how do you like it?" Nikki pressed. "That's what really matters."

"It's weird," Kristen started to answer. "I mean, whenever I look in the mirror I have a hard time believing I'm looking at me. But then I think about it and I realize I'm just not used to it yet. But yeah, I guess I do like it. I've never felt so stylish before."

Both Abbi and Nikki gave Kristen a look up and down. They disagreed that she was stylish, but at least her new hair was a step in the right direction. Still, they had once been on Kristen's path. They were not about to put her down and get her to stop. If anything, they were going to do the opposite, become even more friendly so that Kristen would continue her journey.

"We're glad to hear you like it," Abbi said. "Who was your stylist at Magic Woman?"

At that point the trio's conversation turned into Kristen describing her visit to the salon and the women she met there. Kristen's new friends were interested to hear everything she had to say, especially about Gabby. They both seemed a little in awe of Gabby's lifestyle. Admittedly, so was Kristen. She had never met anyone like her before.

"So what are you having done next?" Nikki asked.

"I wasn't planning on anything," Kristen admitted. "I figured I'd keep going back for regular touch ups on my hair, but other than that, I'm not someone who spends a lot of money on myself."

"Oh, but you have to," Nikki blurted out.

"What Nikki means is you want to take the next step before your next date, don't you?" Abbi said calmly. "I really recommend the Advanced Beauty Lift. It's worth every cent. And I'm certain Blake will be impressed. You'll have him wondering why he even bothered to leave town when he could have stayed here with you."

Kristen's eyes glazed over as she imagined Blake getting tongue-tied when she showed up at the restaurant in a little black dress. She did not even know all of what the Advanced Beauty Lift did, but considering what the Basic Beauty Lift had done for her, the idea of going even further was appealing.

"That does sound nice," Kristen eventually said. "I suppose I can see about taking the next step this weekend."

"You won't regret it," Nikki said.

"Thanks for the advice," Kristen finally said. "But I need to get back to work. Talk to you two later."

The trio parted ways and Kristen returned to her cubicle. However, before she logged back onto her computer, she took a moment and called Magic Woman, making an appointment for the Advanced Beauty Lift package. She would need to look up the details on what it entailed later.

This time, when Kristen stepped into Magic Woman, she did so with a confidence she had never felt before.

"Hi, Penny," she said as she approached the receptionist at the front desk. "I'm here for my appointment."

"Kristen, you're right on time," Penny said as she checked Kristen off on the computer schedule.

The hour was not nearly as early this time, although Kristen had still selected a morning appointment. Penny had recommended it, just to make sure there was plenty of time to complete everything. Kristen had no idea how long her appointment was supposed to last, but she had cleared her Saturday schedule for this. Not that her schedule had been full. She had planned to start reading a new book, but that could also be put off until Sunday.

"I'll go get Gabby for your appointment," Penny said as she got up from her seat behind the desk. Her outfit was similar to the week before, but this time it was blue instead of red. The dress also featured a zipper down the front and she had left it slightly unzipped at the top. It was unclear whether the zipper kept slipping down because of the size of her breasts or if she wore it that way to give that appearance. Either way, Penny's breasts were impressive in their size and it was clear she enjoyed showing them off.

Penny disappeared in the back as Kristen sat down. Last time she had just sat there, waiting. This time, feeling more comfortable with the whole situation, she idly picked up a magazine on the side table and started leafing through it. Kristen had never been one to read fashion magazines. She had never touched them when she visited her old salon, but that had been before she had realized that she had the potential to be stylish. That knowledge made the magazine much more interesting.

"I'm ready for you Kristen," Gabby said as she appeared through the door, a step behind Penny who returned to her seat behind the front desk.

Kristen popped up and followed her stylist to the now familiar booth. She immediately took her seat before she started to speak. "Go out anywhere fun last night?"

Gabby smiled. "Last night was pretty tame by my recent standards. I hit two clubs, didn't meet anyone fun, but still had a good time. I actually got home early enough to take a nap before I got in this morning."

The only difference Kristen could see in Gabby's appearance from last time, was the shift in her hair and makeup. She looked more put together and less like she had been up all night. Then again, she had not been up all night.

"Can't stay out every night," Kristen said.

"But I can always try," Gabby countered. "Now, let's see. Your hair still looks great. And your nose and cheekbones look like they did when you left last week. That's good. Sometimes things don't fully take on the first try, but your body seems pretty adaptable. That's a good thing, by the way. It makes my job a lot easier."

It was only as Gabby went over the changes that had

come from the Basic Beauty Lift that Kristen realized that her nose and cheekbones had changed. It had not just been the makeup. Whatever Gabby had done, her nose and cheekbones had been permanently altered.

Kristen's heart started to pound in her chest. Adrenaline shot through her veins, putting her on high alert. Her fight or flight instinct was kicking in.

"Relax, Kirsten," Gabby said as she placed a comforting hand on Kristen's shoulder. "You're safe here. Nothing bad can happen to you here."

Kristen looked down to see her hands gripping the end of the arm rests, her knuckles turning white. She took a deep breath and forced her hands to relax.

"Sorry," Kristen said. "I don't know what came over me."

"You have nothing to be sorry about," Gabby said. "You actually might be surprised that we get that reaction a lot here. Our methods aren't like other salons. With our backers, we are able to take things a step further than most spas and salons. And sometimes the prospect of permanent changes like we perform here can be daunting, especially for someone new like you."

"Wait, last week's appointment was permanent?" Kristen asked, more in surprise than in anger. "I thought it was all just temporary."

"Kristen, in this line of work, nothing is permanent. But if you're worried about having to keep coming back to get your roots touched up, you don't need to worry about that. Your hair will grow this new color until you decide you want us here at Magic Woman to change it. That's the beauty of all this. The sky really is the limit here."

"Hmm," Kristen said, thinking. She was not sure what to make of this latest news. It had probably been in the fine print of the documents she had signed. Like most people, she never actually read those agreements. Kristen might have been mad if she had disliked her new look, but the truth was, she was growing to like it. She was growing to like it a lot.

"All right. If you're up to it, I can get started on your Advanced Beauty Lift. Now, fair warning, most of today's procedures will be for your body. I'm talking things like nails and skin stuff, maybe give you a bit of a tan, nothing major. Would you prefer tan lines or not?"

"Tan lines?" Kristen asked, trying to keep up. Her mind was awash in various hormones, some telling her to relax, others telling her to run. It was all very confusing. "I guess, not."

"Our minds think alike on that one," Gabby said. "One last question. Do you have a preference on nail polish color?"

"Um," Kristen said, trying to formulate an answer. The truth was she rarely if ever painted her nails. She could not even remember the last time she had done it.

"I was thinking a nice bright red, something to match the lipstick we used last time. How does that sound?"

"Sure, that sounds nice," Kristen said, already beginning to feel relaxed as she let her head fall back in the chair and allowed Gabby to get to work.

Kristen had wanted to be early to the coffee shop for their first date, but for the second one she intentionally arrived late. She was not overly late, but she planned her arrival so that Blake could watch her cross the restaurant wearing her new dress and shoes. Kristen could not believe how good she looked. Gabby had done wonders with her body.

Blake and Kristen had not seen each other since their last date. Blake had been gone. Even Abbi had miscalculated how long he would be gone for. He returned Wednesday, his trip getting extended five extra days. He had returned Wednesday afternoon, arriving at the office in a flurry of papers that needed his signature.

That had been yesterday and Kristen had barely been able to keep it together at work. She kept looking out the entrance of her cubicle to see if she could spot him. The distractions certainly lowered her efficiency on the day, but she figured no one would mind if it happened once. Her work schedule was not supposed to pick up again until later in the quarter. It was still January.

Not that Kristen should have been expecting Blake to appear within sight of her cubicle. They worked on completely different floors of the building. They had a small chance of running into each other in the elevators, but those odds were especially small, considering there were eight different elevators that served the building and she did not know his schedule.

Kristen felt especially good about her return visit to Magic Woman. The work Gabby had done left her feeling almost like a whole new woman. When she was home, Kristen enjoyed running her hands across her bare skin. That was something she had always enjoyed after shaving her legs. The smoothness felt so good. Now, however, her whole body felt that way. Every hair on her body, at least below the neck, had been removed. And as far as Kristen could tell, the smoothness she now enjoyed was permanent.

Admittedly, Kristen was still getting used to having her pubic hair gone. She had always kept herself neatly trimmed, but she had never had the confidence to do away with it entirely. However, Kristen had spent more time staring at her nude reflection in the mirror since Saturday's appointment than she cared to admit.

In addition to her body hair being permanently removed, Kristen's skin looked better than it ever had. Even the scars on her knees from when she fell a few times as a kid were gone. Every imperfection seemed to have been eliminated. Coupled with the light tan, Kristen sometimes felt that her body had been switched for another one. She was certainly not complaining. She approved of all of those changes.

The only thing she struggled with was her nails. Kristen had never been someone who had long nails. She had never grown hers out, preferring to keep them short and professional. Nor had she ever gotten fake nails. The whole concept had never been one that appealed to her.

When she and Gabby had discussed color, they never discussed length. Not that Kristen had been in any state to complain when she left Magic Woman Saturday afternoon. In fact, she had thought little of it until she arrived at work Monday morning and discovered her now long nails made typing a bit difficult. Worse, from what Kristen could tell, these were not fake nails. They were her nails, artificially grown to be longer, much as her hair had grown the week before. However, even though they were her own nails, she was too scared to try and cut them. She was afraid something bad might happen if she cut them. She would just have to adapt to their new length.

Kristen wanted to imagine that she walked gracefully across the restaurant to meet Blake, but as she made her way, she felt more like she was tottering along in her high heels. The dress and shoes had been purchased on the suggestion of Abbi and Nikki. They had been impressed with Kristen's results from her latest trip to Magic Woman and they wanted to further push things along by making sure that Kristen was appropriately dressed for her dinner date.

The little black dress Kristen wore was just about perfect. It was low cut enough to make it clear that she was not a prude, but high enough that she was not at risk of falling out of it. The hem was definitely shorter than Kristen would have liked. It barely reached the middle of her thigh. However, Abbi and Nikki had been insistent when she made the purchase online that this was the dress for her.

Seeing Blake's eyes as she watched her cross the restaurant, Kristen knew she had made the right choice on the dress. Abbi and Nikki did have good fashion sense. And they had not been wrong to steer her toward Magic Woman. That place really did perform magic. However, she wished she had stood up for herself when it came to ordering the shoes. They fit perfectly, but the heels were far too high for Kristen's taste. And for her experience. They were the tallest heels she had ever worn, by a lot. They made walking difficult.

"Hi," Kristen said when she finally arrived at the table. "Sorry I'm a little late."

"You're fashionably late," Blake countered as he got up to take Kristen's coat and help her into her seat. "Which means you're not late at all. And to be honest, looking like that, you made the right call. I couldn't keep my eyes off you as you walked in."

"I'm glad you approve," Kristen said. "I wasn't sure if I was going overboard or not."

"Definitely not," Blake said. "And I think every man in this restaurant would agree with me. I wasn't the only person unable to keep their eyes off of you."

Kristen blushed, but the giddiness she had felt at various times over the past almost two weeks returned. It felt good to be desired.

"You have no idea how much I missed you since our last date," Blake said as he settled in and poured Kristen a glass of wine. "I hope you don't mind, but I took the opportunity to order for both of us already."

"How did you know I wasn't going to stand you up?" Kristen asked. "I was late, after all."

"I wasn't going to be worried until I had finished dessert."

That had not really answered Kristen's question, but then again, she had not worded it in the right way. For her, ordering food for two, but not having the other person show up, would have been a major annoyance. And at a restaurant like this, with the white table cloths and full array of silver-ware and glasses, such a cost would have put a serious dent in her checkbook. But for Blake, it was an acceptable loss.

The pair quickly fell into lively conversation, although it was a bit difficult to avoid talking about work. Much of

Blake's last two weeks had been spent away on business. He was able to fill her in on some of his leisure activities and the different restaurants he got to sample from. However, it was a relief to hear that he had most enjoyed sitting by the hotel pool and reading a book. Kristen felt as if that gave them something in common, something that traversed the socioeconomic divide between them. That alone was enough to make Kristen glad she had gone through all of this. Blake was a great guy and she counted herself lucky to get to know him, even if nothing long term came of it.

* * *

Dinner and dessert had come to a close and Kristen was happily buzzed, the wine adding to what had thus far been a perfect evening. She had fully enjoyed herself with Blake. And it had not hurt that he could not keep his eyes off of her. She even caught him staring when she briefly excused herself to visit the restroom.

"You're not driving home, are you?" Blake asked as he helped her put her coat on. It was cold in January.

"I did a ride share," Kristen answered. "I didn't want to drive home drunk or have to pick my car up here at the restaurant tomorrow."

"Smart thinking," Blake said. "But you know, I can give you a ride home. That is if you want?"

Kristen stood there thinking for a moment. The answer was obvious. She did not want to part ways with Blake just yet. It had been torture waiting for him to return from his trip. She wanted to spend every available second with him while she still could. However, she took her time, wanting to make sure that it was not the alcohol pushing her into a situation she could not control.

"That would be nice. Thank you."

Blake held out his arm and Kristen gratefully accepted it as she led her out of the restaurant and toward his car.

His car, as it turned out, was a fancy blue sports car. That should not have surprised Kristen, given how much money he made, but she had been expecting something a little less ostentatious. This car, whatever it was, looked like it belonged on a racetrack and not on the city streets.

"I hope you don't mind, but I just got this recently and I've been driving it everywhere I can manage. Although I don't take it to work, because I don't like showing off to people who make so much less than me."

Kristen nodded her head as Blake helped her into the low-slung sports car. The entire interior looked like it had come out of a science fiction movie or at least out of a NASA rocket. It got even stranger when Blake turned it on and there was no sound.

"It's electric," Blake said, answering Kristen's unasked question.

Blake pulled the car out of the parking lot and took off down the road in the approximate direction of Kristen's home.

"I was thinking," Blake said as they were stopped at a stoplight. "I could take you home right now or you could come over to my place for a drink. It's your choice."

The wheels in Kristen's head started turning as soon as Blake made the offer. Did she want to go home with Blake, at least for another drink? That answer was obvious. Yes, she wanted that. However, was Kristen willing to take the next logical step. Was she willing to go home with him for more than a drink? As Kristen ran her hand along her bare thing, enjoying the smooth sensation of her skin, a tingle developed deep inside of her. It was a tingle she knew well. And it made her answer even easier.

"Let's have that drink," Kristen answered with a

knowing smile. Even if Blake was just asking her home to have a drink with him, he would get that and so much more.

After seeing Blake's car, she was not surprised to see his house. She honestly did not know why he had bought such a large house for himself, given that he was single and lived alone. It did provide him lots of space. The gated drive was at least a quarter mile long, making for a beautiful drive up to the house.

But it was when Blake pulled his car into the garage that she understood why he had purchased the house. It was just as much about the barn that had been converted into a garage as it was the house and property itself. He needed a place to store all his toys. Kristen had no idea Blake was such a motoring enthusiast. Not that she minded. She was actually happy to see he had additional hobbies he had yet to share with her.

"Do you have a preference on what you'd like to drink?" Blake asked as they entered the living room. Kristen barely heard the question as her head turned back and forth, taking in everything she saw. The living room was as big as her whole apartment. And the big windows that looked out the back, likely provided a great view, even if nothing could be seen in the dark.

"Um, whatever you're having," Kristen said. "I'm not picky."

She did not actually care about what they drank together. She was more interested in what came after. The tingle she had felt in the car had only gotten stronger. Sex was definitely on the menu now.

It did not take long before Blake and Kristen were seated on the couch. Gentle music was playing. Blake gently stroked Kristen's thigh. She parted her legs, pulling the hem of her dress just a little higher.

"Do you have any idea how much I want you right now?" Blake whispered into Kristen's ear.

Her breath caught in her throat at his confession. The tingle had now turned into a burning heat.

"Do you have any idea how hard it is not to rip that dress off of you and take you right here?"

Kristen felt lightheaded, but she knew this was not from the alcohol. This was her body screaming at her, demanding exactly what Blake was offering. Her body wanted him. And the truth was, so did her mind. It was just a little slower to come to that complete realization.

"I want you too," Kristen moaned as Blake kissed her neck.

Blake said nothing as he jumped into action. Before Kristen knew it, he was in Blake's arms. He was carrying her, one arm under her legs and the other behind her back. Her head swam at the sudden movement, leaving her to wrap her arms around the back of Blake's neck and hold on.

Moments later, Kristen found herself laying back on a bed, Blake standing over her. Her hair pooled around her head, creating a halo effect with her blonde hair. She shifted her body, pulling her knees up as she pulled at the hem of her dress, revealing the black thong she had been forced to wear to prevent her underwear from showing from underneath the dress. It was one of the few times in her life she had worn such underwear.

However, Blake seemed to hesitate before making his next move. Kristen was ready for him. She wanted him more than she could have imagined when he showed up at her cubicle just over two weeks ago. She had never jumped into bed with a man this soon in a relationship before, but she had no regrets about doing it now. Everything about this moment seemed right.

"Just to make things perfectly clear," Blake said, his voice serious. "You want this, not because of our respective positions at the company, but because we are two consenting adults in a mature relationship and you expect no favors outside of our relationship together."

"No favors," Kristen moaned. "I just want you."

"Just making sure," Blake said as he started to remove his shirt.

Kristen pulled at her dress, but her eyes were locked on Blake as he disrobed. It turned out he was even more attractive without his shirt on. No wonder he had been able to carry to the bedroom so easily. He was ripped. Those hours playing basketball had clearly paid off.

As Blake finally shucked off his pants, Kristen was pulling her dress up over her head, revealing her thong and bra, both black to match her dress. With both of them in their underwear, Blake kneeled on the bed and leaned over Kristen. He gently held her head as he kissed her.

Kristen returned the kiss with wild abandon. Her body had never wanted a man so much in her life and she had no qualms about getting out of the way and letting her body do its thing. Soon their tongues were dancing in each other's mouths and they were well on their way.

As they kissed, Blake carefully undid the clasp of Kristen's bra. She hardly noticed when he slipped it off her chest. However, once they broke the kiss, she took a moment to look down and revel in the fact she had no tan lines. That had been a good choice.

"Are you ready?" Blake asked as he removed his underwear, revealing his hard cock.

Kristen gasped when she saw it. He was much bigger than any man she had ever been with before. For the briefest of moments she wondered if he would fit inside her, but she pushed that thought away, not wanting to think about it.

"I'm more than ready, stud," Kristen said as she reached

forward and caressed his cock with her hands, being careful to not scratch him with her nails. These things took practice.

"Good," Blake said as he grabbed hold of her thong and pulled hard.

Kristen's butt came up off the bed as the thong slipped down around her legs, revealing her hairless mound and pink pussy. Her juices were already flowing and coated her pussy lips.

With her thong discarded on the floor, Blake crawled up onto the bed, his cock hanging between his legs.

"What do you want?" he asked before he kissed Kristen again.

"I want you," Kristen said after the kiss. "I want your cock."

Kristen had never used such language with any of her sexual partners before. She would have shocked herself had she not already been so aroused and caught up in the moment.

"How can I say no to that?" Blake laughed as he gave Kristen exactly what she wanted. His cock pushed into her waiting entrance, sliding inside her, filling her channel with more cock than she had ever taken before.

"Oh fuck," Kristen moaned as she was hit with a wave of pleasure. However, that wave was only a foreshadowing of what was still to come.

Blake set up a steady rhythm to start, thrusting in and out of Kristen's wet pussy. The waves of pleasure only got stronger each time he pushed into her. Kristen squealed and moaned as each wave hit her brain. Even if they had stopped right there with neither of them cumming, Kristen already knew this was the best sex she had ever had. And the best part was it was not over yet.

As Blake continued his work, Kristen wrapped her arms around his back, her nails scratching him, but neither of them noticed. They were both lost to the erotic moment, living in ecstasy as they fully enjoyed their coupling.

"I'm going to cum," Blake announced as he reached his point of no return.

"Do it," Kristen begged. "I want you to cum inside me."

It was hard for Blake to say no to that. And so he did just as Kristen asked. He buried himself inside her one last time as his cock surged with cum. A moment later he was shooting rope after rope of hot white cum deep into her pussy as he came.

Kristen was cumming too, those pleasure waves now forming a rapid cascade that filled every part of her body. She screamed out in erotic ecstasy as half the nerve fibers in her body fired off in pleasure.

She had never felt this way before. Sex had always been pleasurable, but nothing like this. Kristen was already certain she was hooked. She could never go back to the way things were before. Blake had opened her eyes to what was possible and she never wanted to let him go. She might not yet be in love with him, but she was definitely in lust with him. And she would do almost anything to keep him as long as he kept making her feel like that.

As the pair cuddled following their coupling, Kristen could not help but smile. Then again, neither could Blake. They were both very happy with the choices they had made that night and they both hoped this night would be followed with many more like it.

8

There were only two people at the office who noticed that both Kristen and Blake were late to work the morning following their dinner date. Those two people were Abbi and Nikki.

And in the subsequent days and weeks, they had inserted themselves into Kristen's life to the point where she happily accepted their invitation to go shopping together. Of course, it was getting harder to keep the budding office romance a secret. They had more than once been spotted either leaving work, or arriving at work, together. Sometimes it was just easier to organize their transportation that way as the pair continued to date.

Not only had Kristen and Blake continued to go on dates, they made that first night together only one of many. Even though Kristen had not spent the night with Blake that first night, they had broken that barrier after their next date, with Kristen spending the night at Blake's house.

Admittedly, theirs was a relationship that always saw her spend the night at Blake's house. Her small apartment simply could not compare and she did not want to let him see all that she used to be. And so much of Kristen had changed since Blake first asked her out. She had made several significant upgrades to her wardrobe, in addition to her two appointments she had made at Magic Woman.

And true to Gabby's word, everything that she had gone through was permanent. The nails, the tan, the lack of body hair, even the color of her hair, all seemed permanent. The only reason Kristen had returned to Magic Woman was for a traditional hair appointment. Surprisingly, they did those in addition to everything else.

While Kristen ultimately had Blake to thank for asking her out, she did need to thank her two new friends. Abbi and Nikki were so far ahead of her in every aspect, that it was sometimes daunting to think that she belonged among their company. However, she could not deny that they had served as good friends and even better fashion consultants. Kristen never bought a new dress or pair of shoes without consulting one or both of them first.

Thus, it became completely natural for the three of them to go out shopping together. But unlike other shopping trips, this one had a specific purpose. They were all going out on a triple date to a club. There would be dancing. It was all very fancy and Kristen needed desperate help so that she had something appropriate to wear.

Somewhere along the line, Kristen realized that her two friends were not only working for Darren and Mike, but that they were dating them too. There was a time when that information would have shocked her. Instead, now, it just made her more comfortable in her position with Blake. If Darren and Mike could get away with dating their secretaries, there was no reason she could not be with Blake.

"We're going to have so much fun Saturday night," Nikki gushed as they entered the shop.

"You're going to love the Seven Club," Abbi added. "The

food is delicious and the music is amazing. They have a live band every night of the week and sometimes they had other acts, comics and whatnot. And everyone there is usually rich or famous."

"Sounds impressive," Kristen said, sounding less enthusiastic as her friends. Dating Blake had opened her to new experiences and to places she had never dreamed of getting into before, but it also reminded her that he was wealthy and she was not. The only way she had managed to keep her spending in check was by the fact that she ate so many meals with Blake these days, with him buying. And even then, she found herself dipping into her savings, including on this shopping trip to buy a dress. There was no way the money she saved on her grocery bill in a month could pay for her dress.

Kristen knew none of this was sustainable. At some point she would need to have a talk with Blake about it. Either they would need to go to places that she did not need to dress up for or he would need to start helping her pay for her wardrobe additions. The problem was, Kristen liked her new clothes so much more than her old clothes and she was usually too proud to admit she needed help. She had been raised to be an independent woman and that should have meant she could afford paying her own way. And if Blake were another accountant like her, she might have been able to manage that. But when she was perched on Blake's arm at a fancy restaurant or at the Seven Club, she needed to look the part. Gabby at Magic Woman had been a huge help, but there was more to looking good than having a great body and great hair. She needed to dress in a way that fit the part and that cost money.

"Is there anything you're looking forward to about the date night?" Abbi asked as they browsed the shop, looking for the perfect dress.

"I don't know," Kristen answered. "To be honest, I'm pretty nervous about the whole thing. I don't think I've ever felt that I'm on the wrong side of the tracks with this. I've heard stories about the Seven Club and I never imagined in my wildest dreams I would ever get to go there."

"Don't be nervous," Nikki said sympathetically. "Everyone there is just like us. Yes, some of them have money, but not all of them. It's all about who you know and you know someone really special."

"I'll have to take your word for it," Kristen said, still not feeling confident in the whole thing.

"You know what you need?" Abbi interjected. "Magic Woman has the perfect thing for you. Their Mental Relaxation package will do you wonders. Trust me. Both Nikki and I have done it. We went in worrying about stuff like what bad stuff could happen if we started dating the men we work for. And you know what? Afterward, no more worries. It's great."

"Totally," Nikki agreed. "I'm thinking about going in for the Baby Makeover soon. That's my next step and even though I haven't booked it yet, I can't wait."

"I suppose I could do that," Kristen said as she tried to decide if her credit cards could handle buying a dress, with the accompanying shoes, and making another visit to Magic Woman. In the end, however, the answer was simple.

9

Kristen walked into Magic Woman with a measure of trepidation about what she was about to do. She had come to terms with what had been done to her body thus far. In fact, she had no complaints whatsoever about the services she had thus far received. However, the idea that her mind could somehow be altered bothered her.

Despite those fears, she still made her appointment and showed up on time. Kirsten felt compelled to do this. She needed to fit in better with Blake, as well as with Abbi and Nikki. And having a more relaxed attitude would not hurt her any. In fact, it seemed like it would help her. The tension she felt from her days at work would not build up in the same way, forcing her to spend time alone decompressing. She could be spending that time with Blake.

If there was any question left, it was that she definitely loved the man. Blake was quickly becoming her everything. That only left how Blake felt. He had not been as forthcoming with his feelings as she had. That bothered Kristen. The more she gave to the relationship, the more power Blake had over her. She had always expected an equal partnership with a man and not having that worried her.

"Hi, Kristen," Penny said with a smile. "Welcome back."

"Thanks, Penny," Kristen said with a smile. As worried as she was about all of this, she did enjoy her visits to Magic Woman. She might not have thought much of Penny the first time they had met, but Kristen had changed her mind since then. Penny was like an always shining ray of sunshine. And she looked really sexy too. "Your boobs are looking bigger. Did you have work done?"

"Gabby did them for me," Penny said with delight as she gave her shoulders a little shimmy. Her boobs jiggled in her low-cut top.

"They look great," Kristen said. And they did. And seeing Penny certainly helped allay her trepidations about what she was about to go through.

There had been a time when Kristen never would have asked Penny about her breasts or complimented them in the way she had. However, after spending more and more time with Abbi and Nikki, such topics of conversation had become more normal for her. Fashion had become a growing interest for Kristen and along with that came what lay under those clothes, breasts chief among them.

"Thank you," Penny said, still smiling, but now wider following Kristen's compliment. "I'll let Gabby know you're here."

Kristen sat down and immediately picked up a magazine and began reading. The women she saw in the pictures reminded her so much of Abbi and Nikki. And more and more, they reminded her of herself. Kristen was not that far away from looking like the models in some of the pictures. She almost admitted that with a little more work, she could be a model, but she stopped herself short. Modeling might appear appealing, but Kristen did not have an interest. Her reasons for looking as she did was not to pose in front of a camera, but to look good hanging on Blake's arm.

"Looking great, Kristen," Gabby said as she stepped into her client's line of vision.

Kristen followed a long pair of legs, perched on sky-high heels, up to an impossibly short skirt. Then there was bare skin before a barely there bra top, followed finally by Gabby's familiar face and blonde hair.

"Thanks," Kristen said as she put the magazine down and followed Gabby into the back.

"You're taking the next step, I see," Gabby said. "I approve."

"Next step?" Kristen asked, confused.

"Generally our clients follow a specific path with our services," Gabby explained. "You started out like many women with the Basic Beauty Lift. Then you moved on to the Advanced Beauty Lift. The next step on that path is the Mental Relaxation."

"I see," Kristen said. "Do you mind telling me what I'm getting myself into? Admittedly you don't have much information about them online. If I weren't so happy with the results from the first two packages, I might have been mad at the permanent nature of the changes."

"I've never met a woman who isn't happy with what we do here," Gabby said with a knowing smile. "As for what we're about to do today, think of it as a spa day. You'll get a massage. You'll get to soak in a special warm bath. And the whole time you'll be fitted with a special cap that helps stimulate the certain hormone production in your brain to help stabilize your mood. I guarantee, when you leave here today, you'll feel like a million bucks."

"Good, because I'm going to the Seven Club with my boyfriend on a triple date," Kristen said, satisfied with Gabby's answer.

Gabby led Kristen deeper into the building, past her usual booth and eventually into a small room with a bench and several locker-like cubbies.

"You can get undressed in here," Gabby explained. "There is a robe if you want to wear one. You don't have to. Then you go though the orange door where you will get to soak in a special hot bath. I'll come collect you for your massage. Then you get another soak after that. Oh, and before I forget, please wear this cap on your head throughout your stay."

Gabby pulled what looked like a yellow swimmer's cap off a shelf. However, this cap looked a bit more high tech. It featured several wires sticking out of it and lots of little bumps all across the outside. The inside looked smooth as expected.

Kristen pulled on the cap first, before Gabby left, just to make sure she had it on correctly.

"Yes, perfect," Gabby said. "I'll see you in a little bit. Enjoy your soak."

Kristen quickly disrobed as soon as Gabby had left the room. She hung up her clothes in an empty cubby. It seemed unlikely that anyone would steal her clothes. They were not nearly as fashionable as the employees' clothes and they were not very valuable. Kristen then donned the provided robe and opened the door that Gabby had indicated.

As soon as the door was open, Kristen was inundated with hot and steamy conditions. She stepped forward, barely able to see more than a few feet in front of her.

"Hello?" she called out, just in case there was someone in the room. Not that she could hear anyone. In fact, all she could hear was the patter of her own feet on the tiled floor and what sounded like running water, possibly a fountain or small waterfall.

It took a few moments for Kristen to acclimate to her surroundings. She located a pool of water in the center of the room. The water bubbled like a jacuzzi, producing the heat and steam that filled the room.

Only a minute or so after donning her robe, Kristen was shrugging it off again, letting it call a few feet from the edge of the tub. She then carefully stepped into the water.

"Oh, that's nice," Kristen said as she slowly lowered herself into the pool of water. It was the perfect temperature, straddling the line between warm and hot.

Finding a built-in bench, Kristen sat down, the water just covering her shoulders. She let her body relax. As it turned out, her mind was doing the same thing, aided by the contraption on her head. It did not just keep her hair from getting wet, but it helped facilitate the relaxation of her mind, clearing out all those pesky worries and anxieties.

It did not take long for Kristen to lose all track of time. She was simply present in the moment. The past, the future, none of it seemed to matter to her. And even the present felt a lot more simple than it ever had before.

However, nothing like that can last forever. Before Kristen knew it, Gabby had stepped into the pool room and woke Kristen from her almost trance-like state.

"It's time for your massage," Gabby said.

"Already?" Kristen asked, surprised by how quickly the time seemed to have passed. She could have asked what time it was, but that seemed unneeded. If Gabby said it was time for her massage, who was she to argue?

"It is," Gabby answered. "And I think you'll like your masseuse. Penny has been asking for more responsibilities. She actually came to us as a licensed massage therapist. You'll be in good hands."

That was enough to get Kristen out of the pool. She did not seem to mind that she was naked in front of Gabby. After all, she had Gabby to thank for her improved features. However, since there did not seem to be any towels around for Kristen to use, she did end up putting her robe back on. It soaked up much of the water that had not already beaded on Kristen's smooth skin and simply slid off her body.

"All set?" Gabby asked.

"Uh huh," Kristen nodded. The hot bath had already done wonders for her relaxation. Her body felt heavenly. A massage would only emphasize all of that.

"Perfect," Gabby said. "This way."

Gabby led Kristen through another door and into a small room. In the center was a massage table covered in towels.

"Go ahead and hop up on the table and I'll go get Penny. You can hang up your robe on the wall."

As soon as Gabby closed the door behind her, Kristen did as she was instructed. She once again shrugged off the robe and hung it up on the wall. Then she climbed up onto the massage table and laid face down. Normally there was a blanket or towel for her to climb under, but that absence did not bother her. She was too relaxed to care about that.

A moment later there was a knock on the door and Penny entered with her beaming smile.

"Hi, Penny," Kristen said almost groggily.

"I'm so excited I get to finally do more than just work the front desk," Penny said enthusiastically. She had changed out of the clothes Kristen had seen her wearing at the front desk, opting instead for a bikini top, which did little to hide her large breasts, and a short skirt that barely covered the curve of her ass. She was still perched on high heels though. It seemed Penny never went anywhere without wearing heels.

Kristen said nothing as Penny slowly readied herself for the massage. She started by connecting a cable that had been stashed below the table and connecting it to the wires sticking out of Kristen's cap. She paid this no attention, not understanding the process and feeling just fine with that fact. Kristen did not need to understand everything. She trusted

Penny, Gabby, and all the other women at Magic Woman that she had yet to meet.

However, as Kristen laid there while Penny finished getting ready, including covering her hands in massage oil, she felt a throbbing in her head. She thought little of it. The throbbing was not painful. It just was there. Little did Kristen understand that the throbbing was a result of the cable attached to her cap, priming her brain for new inputs.

Kristen noticed none of this once the massage started. Even the throbbing seemed to go away.

"Let me know if there's any muscles you want me to focus on," Penny said as she started massaging Kristen's back. "Or if there's anything else you think I should know. I always love getting massages. They're so relaxing. But it's more than that. Can I tell you a secret? I always get turned on when I get a massage."

Just at that moment, Penny leaned over a bit more than was necessary and let her large breasts rub against Kristen's back and across her exposed butt. Kristen did not say anything, but she certainly felt it. There was a familiar tingle building inside of her. She was growing aroused, just as Penny had mentioned.

The massage went on for a long time. Penny was very thorough and she kept talking the whole time. Kristen zoned out for much of it, but her brain remained receptive to the comments, taking them in, even if only at a subconscious level.

And by the end, there was no doubt in Kristen's mind that she was horny. The few thoughts that seemed to permeate her mind were all about getting herself off at the next opportunity. It was the last bit of tension she needed to release.

"We're all done here," Penny said as she unhooked the cable from Kristen's cap. "You can go into the next room and have another nice soak. Gabby will be by to collect you when it's time for you to get out."

Kristen did not say anything, but she followed Penny's directions. She was in no mood to disagree with such simple orders. And if she was lucky, the soak would give her a chance to get herself off. That was important. Then she would finally be completely and totally relaxed, just like she was supposed to be. And then it would only be a matter of getting ready for her date at the Seven Club. With the dress Abbi and Nikki had helped her pick out, she knew she was going to look great hanging onto Blake's arm.

However, as Kristen got up from the massage table, she did not bother to retrieve her robe. She was now so relaxed that concerns about people seeing her naked were simply gone from her mind. It was easier to just go into the next room and return to her soaking. After all, Gabby had said she did not actually need the robe. And now that she was two-thirds of the way through her latest appointment at Magic Woman, she was in agreement.

10

After finishing her appointment at Magic Woman, Kristen felt amazing. She had never felt so relaxed. And it was not just her body that felt relaxed, although she had never felt her body so loose before. Her mind felt slow and sated, not unlike after she had just had an orgasm. Then again, she had taken a few minutes to get herself off while soaking in the final tub. She had simply been too turned on to not touch herself in the last hot tub.

Following her time at Magic Woman, Kristen drove straight out to Blake's house. They decided she could get ready there before driving into town to pick up the other two couples. It also meant she could stay at his house that night without having to worry about where her car was or bothering Blake to drive her somewhere else. It was for the best all around.

Kristen was not sure what it was, but she struggled to get herself ready to go as quickly as she usually managed. She might be in the middle of applying makeup and then she would just stop, her mind wandering into nothing. Luckily, she had left herself plenty of time. There were no concerns about them being late. However, when Kristen did finish, she discovered there was a car waiting for them out front.

"I decided it would be fun if we all rode in a limo tonight," Blake said. He looked stunning in his black tuxedo. Even the bow tie was a proper tied knot and not just a clip-on.

"That sounds lovely," Kristen said. As she took hold of Blake's arm as he led her out of the house and out to the car, she almost felt like she was floating. It was a wonderful feeling that a part of her never wanted to end. She did not say that the last time she had been in a limousine was for her high school prom. Somehow, she guessed both she and Blake would be getting luckier this time. Kristen's prom date had snuck in a bottle of alcohol to the prom and then went and got himself so wasted, he could not even get himself hard if Kristen had been willing to have sex with him. His drunken behavior had nixed any hope he had in that department.

This time, however, Kristen was certain it would be different. Her and Blake's sex life was robust and she had no doubts she would be satisfying the tingle that had once again begun to build inside of her. Being with Blake had always made her a little aroused, but it was like the tap had been opened wider since her Mental Relaxation appointment. Her brain was no longer in the way trying to dictate how she should feel.

The limo driver helped both Kristen and Blake into the back of the car. It was a large limo with lots of space for the three couples, but for now it was just the two of them.

"Just think of all the fun we could have back here," Kristen said as she snuggled in next to Blake. Her dress was not exactly warm and she was seeking heat.

"What kind of fun are you thinking of?" Blake asked with a smirk.

"I mean, there's enough room for us to fuck if we wanted," Kristen answered. "Or I could kneel between your legs and suck your cock."

At the mention of sucking Blake's cock, Kristen's face turned red. She had not planned to say those words. She had barely thought them before they were spilling out of her mouth. But it was true. There was definitely room for her to kneel on the floor of the limo and suck Blake's cock if they wanted. Not that blowjobs were a part of their sex routines. Kristen had always thought blowjobs were degrading and gross. A part of her still felt that way, but given how hot she found the whole idea, she was more willing to entertain it.

"I'll have to remember that," Blake said as they neared Darren's home. Rather than go for a big house on the outskirts of town, he had chosen something a little more modest for himself, although the house was still plenty big. It being closer to the center of town had been important to him.

As soon as the limousine pulled up in front of Darren's house, he and Abbi appeared in the doorway. Darren held out his arm and she leaned into him as they descended the front walk.

"Howdy, folks," Darren said as the driver helped him and Abbi into the limo.

Abbi seemed especially giggly and slightly off balance as she took her seat.

"Abbi decided to pre-drink a little tonight," Darren explained. "I'm not sure why she bothered, since none of us are driving and there will be plenty of time to do that later."

"It's fun," Abbi said, giggling.

Kristen was not going to argue with her friend. At least she looked like she was having fun. That was what was important about all of this.

It was a short drive deeper into town to reach Mike's condo building. He had opted to use his wealth to buy a penthouse condo overlooking the river. The wait for him and Nikki took a little longer, but they too soon joined the two other couples already in the limo.

As the car set off once again, Blake began speaking, "Kristen here was commenting that with all the room we have in the back here, she could kneel on the floor and suck my cock."

"Hey, that's an idea," Mike said. "I know I could use a pre-dinner blowjob. What do you say, Nikki?"

However, Nikki was already sliding onto the floor of the limo. So too was Abbi, unable to stop herself in her current state.

Kristen normally would have been horrified to see her two friends go down on their boyfriends in such a manner, at least when there were other people around to watch. But her mind was too relaxed and her body too turned on for the horror to form. Instead, she felt oddly jealous, like she needed to do more to fit in.

"Come on, Kristen," Nikki said.

"This was your idea, you know," Blake added.

She did know and that was what made it weird. As much as such an act seemed like something that should be reserved for the bedroom, or at least when she and Blake were alone together, she could not deny how hot Abbi and Nikki looked as they started to bob their heads.

Suddenly Kristen found herself on the floor of the limo, on her knees. She had not even noticed when she slid down to join her friends. However, it felt good to fit in, to go with the flow, and to do what the rest of her friends were doing. And as soon as her lips were wrapped around Blake's cock, she could almost forget that there were three blowjobs taking place in the back of the limo.

It was a sensation Kristen had never experienced before. She had always viewed blowjobs as degrading for the woman. They were the sort of thing that she was supposed to hate. However, it quickly became apparent that Kristen did not hate having a cock in her mouth. In fact, she discovered that she had a strange sense of power. She controlled Blake's pleasure. She could change her technique or speed to increase his pleasure or she could make a different change and slow things down, teasing him and keeping him on edge.

More importantly, Kristen discovered there was something about the taste of Blake's cock that she liked. There was a manly flavor that she could not describe, but loved. Then there was the taste of pre-cum. Since she had always been anti-blowjob, she had never tasted cum before. To her surprise, it was something she actually liked.

"That's nice," Blake said, throwing his head back as Kristen went to town on his cock. She had seen just enough porn to have an idea of what she should be doing. Blake's grunts and groans provided her with the feedback she needed.

Darren was the first of the trio to cum. He shot his load into Abbi's waiting mouth and she hungrily slurped it down. Mike came next, blasting his seed down Nikki's throat. That only left Blake still to go.

Kristen was aware that she had an audience. Again, she normally would have been horrified, but given what had already happened, she felt proud. She felt like she was finally starting to fit in with her friends. Yes, there was little doubt they were sluts, what with how they liked to dress and the fact they had no qualms with sucking off their boyfriends with company around them. But then again, Kristen was finding herself to be a bit of a slut as well. Her actions on the evening spoke far louder than her words ever could.

"I'm about to cum," Blake announced, providing Kristen warning in case she did not want to taste or swallow his cum. However, she already knew what she wanted. Kristen had been given the smallest of tastes of Blake's cum and she now knew she wanted more of it. Little did she fully comprehend that this was to be the first of many blowjobs and the first of many loads she would be swallowing.

"Yum," Kristen said, licking her lips after she had finished swallowing down Blake's cum.

She looked up at Blake's smiling face. It was not just that he had cum. He was, for the first time, completely satisfied with Kristen as his girlfriend. He had asked her out with an interest for more, yes, but he had always had his doubts. The changes that she had made in her life thus far were great, but he had always wanted just a little bit more. Now the only thing that would make Kristen better in his eyes was if she had a more sizable chest, but he could not argue with any of the rest. And Kristen's breasts were not a deal breaker.

For Kristen, she felt a fulfillment she had not felt before. Maybe it was her currently elevated state of relaxation, but she felt as if she had found her place. She had found a man she loved and there was no better display of devotion than to want to provide him with pleasure while seeking none for herself. And in the end, that fulfillment was more pleasurable than she could have imagined.

* * *

All three women took their time preparing to exit the limo when they arrived at the Seven Club. After the impromptu blowjobs, they all needed to spend some time fixing their makeup, especially their lipstick. Thankfully, their appearances were entirely salvageable and when they each stepped out of the limo in front of the club, they looked as impeccable as they had when they had climbed in.

Kristen had never experienced anything quite like the scene outside the club. There were photographers snapping shots of the people who went in and out. This was the kind of place where rich people and celebrities went for birthday celebrations and other special events. The paparazzi were out in force and all six former occupants of the limo found themselves blinking rapidly as flash bulbs fired off, their pictures getting taken. It was better to take the photo without waiting to figure out if the person was famous enough to sell the photo to a magazine or tabloid.

There had been a time as a kid when Kristen had wondered what it was like at the Seven Club. Everyone knew about it. There were all kinds of stories about the place. The club had existed going back to prohibition, when it had been a speakeasy. Since then, the club had changed locations, needing a larger dining room and dance floor. Its clientele was different too. Instead of accepting anyone who could pay the cover charge and who did not look like a cop, it now required being someone of means to even get a reservation. And between Blake, Darren, and Mike, they had enough means and clout to get a big table for the evening. There would be no hurry to leave after they finished their meals.

Before arriving at the club, Kristen had felt sexy, if a bit exposed in her blue gown. The dress was backless, with two straps that went over her shoulders and wrapped around under her arm and a strap across the back that kept the dress from exposing her small breasts. The skirt portion of the gown had a long slit up the side, exposing most of her leg as she walked or even simply stood. Blake had complimented how she looked in the gown more times than she could count.

However, now that she stood out in front of the club, with her picture getting taken, she felt glamorous for the first time in her life. And, she decided, feeling glamorous felt really good. If this was what being with Blake was like, she was more than happy to take on a subservient role with him to continue to feel this way.

Blake held out his arm to Kristen before he guided her into the club. He led the way, having made the reservation himself. It was his name that they would be asking for.

Stepping inside the club, there was already a live band playing. Blake, Kristen, and the others were shown to their table. It was an out of the way spot, where they would not attract too much attention. Although there was a part of Kristen that was disappointed in that fact. She had suddenly grown to enjoy people looking at her and she wanted that to continue. However, it was much easier to stick with Blake and let him lead the way. If he wanted a more intimate dinner, that was acceptable to her. He was the one paying for her meal after all.

Dinner went better than Kristen could have expected. Blake ordered for her, something she had come to expect with him. She loved the fact she was not asked to interact with the waiter at all. She just had to sit there and look pretty, which she was definitely able to do. As it turned out, Abbi and Nikki were the same way. Their boyfriends did the ordering while they just had to sit there and smile. Although Abbi could not help but sway a little as she sat there, the alcohol she had consumed earlier still affecting her equilibrium.

The service was impeccable and the food was even better. Kristen ate lightly, not wanting her meal to get in the way of dancing later. It had proven to be a fantastic evening thus far, but she did not want to see that ruined by anything bad happening at the end of the evening.

Kristen did pay close attention to how her two friends interacted with their boyfriends. They had already shown her the importance of sucking cock, which she was glad to learn, but there were so many other little, almost imperceptible, behaviors she knew she could learn to be a better girl-friend for Blake. After all, she wanted to fit in with not only her friends, but with the whole scene, whether that was dinner and dancing at the Seven Club or it was a triple date with the three women being as good as friends as the three men.

Before Kristen even realized it, she was parroting many of Abbi and Nikki's movements. She was even starting to talk more like them, on the few occasions when she actually said anything. Then again, Abbi and Nikki were not particu-larly chatty when they were with Darren and Mike. Normally the pair were practically finishing each other's sentences, but when they were with their boyfriends, they shut up, deferring to them for almost everything.

As dinner ended, Abbi and Nikki excused themselves to use the restroom.

"Come on, Kristen," Nikki said. "You need to come too."

"Oh, okay, sure," Kristen said. "Excuse me, honey."

"Sure, babe," Blake said.

As the three women walked away from the table, Nikki whispered, "Swing your ass a bit. They're watching us."

Kristen did as she was beckoned. After all, she wanted to look good for Blake. She wanted him to want her.

In the restroom, the three women ignored the stalls and instead went straight to the mirrors. It was time to touch up their makeup.

"You look like you're having fun tonight," Nikki said.

"Me?" Kristen asked as she touched up her lipstick, applying another thick coat.

"Yeah, I think you like being a sexy girlfriend to Blake," Abbi said, her speech slightly slurred. She seemed more sober than before, but she had been drinking at the same pace as the rest of the table, leaving Kristen confused how she could still be standing. Kristen could definitely feel the lightheadedness that accompanied drinking alcohol. It felt good though, complementing the evening, making her feel just a little more dependent on Blake.

"Maybe I do," Kristen said. "Is that so bad?"

"It's great," Nikki answered. "I'd rather be a sexy girl-friend than some boring accountant."

"Hey," Kristen said in mock anger. "Why can't I be both?"

Both Abbi and Nikki started giggling. "You'll see," Abbi finally said.

The conversation would have bothered Kristen, but by the time the trio returned to the table to rejoin their boyfriends, she had more important things to think about, like dancing. And it was not like she could stay mad at her friends, even if she had been mad. They had been nothing but nice to her since they introduced themselves to her. They were quickly becoming her best friends. Not that Kristen had many friends before.

The rest of the night was filled with dancing. As most of the guests for the evening transitioned away from dinner and toward the dance floor, the band shifted the music it played from relaxing evening fare to something more uptempo and exciting, something Kristen could shake her ass to. She and Blake danced for what felt like hours. It felt a bit like prom should have felt and by the end of the night, she was ready for more than just a ride home. She was ready to ride Blake all night long.

11

Ever since that night at the Seven Club, life for Kristen had changed a lot. She found it more and more difficult to get through her workday.

As an accountant, Kristen needed to follow strict rules on how she recorded financial numbers. It was not just a matter of getting the various sums to add up correctly, but it was the law. She had a legal obligation to do her work in a certain way. The problem arose from the fact that Kristen was less and less interested in remaining so strict. She found herself mentally unprepared to focus for long periods of time. And she certainly did not have the discipline to ensure every detail was perfect.

Instead, Kristen found herself much more interested to just go with the flow. She was much more interested in almost everything other than her work. It did not help that she was spending more time than ever with Blake. She could count the number of nights she had spent in her own bed in the past month on one hand. And all that time had left her wanting even more. It had gotten to the point where Kristen could not stop herself from daydreaming about Blake during the workday. He was always on her mind.

And having Blake always on her mind also tended to make clear another change in Kristen's life. Her libido had taken off like a rocket since that night at the Seven Club. Kristen had thought she had a good sexual relationship with Blake before that night, but now it seemed to be supercharged. There was evening sex, as there had often been, but now there was morning sex too. Whenever she woke up alongside Blake, she could not help herself when she saw his morning wood.

Adding to that, there were also the blowjobs. Kristen had gone from being an oral virgin to almost giving head on command. She had even started climbing under the table at a restaurant one night when Blake joked about her blowing him right then and there. He had to actually order her to retake her seat and promised her she could suck his cock when they got back in the car. Kristen had been insistent that he fulfill his promise.

The warming weather had also changed things for Kristen. Now that she felt good about her body and she wanted to be viewed as sexy, especially by Blake, she had made a few alterations to her style. More of her tops showed off a thin band of bare skin around her middle. She was not going around with a completely bare midriff, but she was certainly willing to show a little tanned skin between the hem of her top and the band of her pants, shorts, or skirt.

Kristen had also followed the lead of her friends, Abbi and Nikki, to button fewer buttons on her work blouses. She also more and more often wore skirts to the office, with heels too. And even the skirts had started to get shorter. She looked more and more like her secretary friends by the week.

However, that all changed when both women made a

return trip to Magic Woman. When they returned from their Baby Makeovers, Kristen could hardly believe her eyes when she saw them. Everything about them had been enhanced. Their breasts were bigger. Their asses were bigger. Their waits were a tiny bit smaller. Their hair was longer and more vibrant. Their lips were more plump. And that was just what was physically different.

Each change by itself, had been small. When taken together, the difference was obvious. But what was even bigger was how their personalities shifted. Abbi and Nikki were no rocket scientists, but they could at least pretend to follow along with a technical conversation. That had ended. They were still wonderful friends and Kristen enjoyed spending time with them, but she had learned to not talk about accounting with them. They simply did not have the patience to sit through such a boring topic without getting bored and trying to change the subject. At best, they would start twirling a lock of hair with their finger and stare off into space.

"You've got to do it," Abbi pushed as the trio were out for happy hour drinks after work.

"Yeah, it's, like, the best," Nikki added enthusiastically.

"I'm thinking about it," Kristen said. And that was the truth. As much as her life had changed and been made more difficult by her choices, she still felt like she did not fit in among her friends. Whenever they all went out like this, or when the men came along for triple dates, Kristen always felt like the odd one out.

On this particular evening, Kristen noticed the difference even more. The weather was warm and the sun was still out. Despite driving to the restaurant straight from work, both Abbi and Nikki had changed out of their tight blouses and short skirts and into even tighter and more revealing tops and skirts. The amount of cleavage on display, between the two of them, was enough to make Kristen very jealous of her friends.

Kristen had never cared about breast size before, but after seeing her friends return from Magic Woman with bigger breasts, she could not help but make the comparison. And their willingness to show off their cleavage, even at work, made it all worse. Deep down, Kristen knew she should not have been jealous of her friends. That, however, did little to assuage the fact she had begun to wonder what it would be like to have bigger breasts. The fact such a thing was next for her at Magic Woman did not help matters. It was more and more becoming a when, not an if.

"Good," Abbi said. "And once you get yourself fixed up, we need to talk about your name."

"What's wrong with my name?" Kristen asked.

"Come on, girl," Nikki said. "You got to spice it up a little."

"Kristen is a nice name," Abbi said. "But it's not a sexy name. Don't you want a sexy name?"

Kristen dropped her shoulders and let her gaze fall into her lap. Yes, of course she wanted that, but she did not feel right about agreeing to it right away. She needed to wait.

"I think Krissi is perfect," Nikki said, nodding her head along to the music playing in the restaurant. "You could do Kristi too, but I like Krissi."

So did Kristen. Abigail had been shortened to Abbi. Nicole had been shortened to Nikki. It only made sense to shorten her name to Krissi.

"I'll think about that too," Kristen said, although she knew this would turn out similar to her decision to return to Magic Woman for her next set of upgrades.

"Well, I'm calling it," Nikki continued. "You're Krissi now. It just feels right."

"I like it," Abbi added. "And before you know it, you'll be upstairs working with us, answering phones and stuff. Hi there, Blake Worthington's office, this is Krissi. How can I direct your call?"

Kristen was silent. This was the moment. She knew it. This was the moment when she decided to embrace this new budding version of herself or she fought back and returned to her former self. The problem was, Kristen actually liked the idea of working with her best friends upstairs, even if it meant a demotion to secretary to make it happen. And she liked the idea of getting the bigger boobs and changing her name to sound sexier. Sure, she would be dumber, but Blake was there to make up for that.

The problem was, it came down to Kristen's love for Blake. That love had only grown stronger with each passing day. They loved each other. And Kristen could feel herself changing to be a better girlfriend and partner. As much as she had once wanted an equal partnership with a man, she had discovered her submissive side and was definitely enjoying it. Kristen had no doubt in her mind that returning to the way things were would mean breaking up with Blake. Just the thought of that made her sick to her stomach. There was no way Kristen could break up with him. Therefore, at some point, she knew she would be calling herself Krissi. It was only a matter of when.

In the meantime, Kristen would hold her tongue and not rush any decisions as she enjoyed the night out with the girls.

"Hi, Kristen," Penny said with a smile as she entered Magic Woman for her latest appointment.

"Hi, Penny. You can call me Krissi now. That's what everyone calls me now."

Kristen had avoided changing her name, but Abbi and Nikki forced her hand. They had started just referring to her as Krissi and anyone who called her Kristen when they were nearby was quickly corrected. Even Blake had started using the name. There might have been a time when she would have told Blake off for that, or even insisted on being called Kristen, but she no longer had it in her. It was so much easier to just go with the flow. If everyone wanted to call her Krissi, especially Blake, how could she argue with that.

And so Kristen officially became Krissi.

"Krissi is a cute name," Penny said. "You can even dot the i's with hearts or stars or something fun like that."

Penny's suggestion reminded Krissi that her friends had started doing exactly that when they returned from their Baby Makeovers at Magic Woman. She wondered if she would be doing the same. After all, Krissi had already come to terms with the fact she would not be the intelligent accountant she had long been when her appointment was over. Not that she was sad about that fact.

Reaching this point had been difficult for Krissi. Abbi and Nikki were clearly in the corner pushing her to go through with it, having made the leap themselves. There had been long talks with Blake.

"I just want you to be happy," Blake had said so many times over the past weeks. And those words were true, but Krissi could not help but feel there was more to it. Whenever they discussed the pros and cons of taking the next step, Blake always seemed more excited about the effects of the Baby Makeover. Having seen what had happened to both Abbi and Nikki, it was obvious he liked what he saw. However, Blake always stressed that her decision would have no impact on their relationship. He would love her no matter what she chose.

However, in the end, it was impossible for Krissi to hold out forever. Between seeing Blake's excitement at the idea of her being a little hotter and a little ditzier and the constant pushing and prodding from her friends, it was only a matter of time before Krissi made the appointment.

"I just might," Krissi finally said about dotting her i's with hearts. "By the way, I just wanted to say I really liked that massage you gave me last time. It was so good I haven't needed one since."

Penny giggled before she responded. "I'm glad to hear it. I don't get to do stuff like that a lot, but it's always fun to pitch in and do more than sit at the front desk."

Little did Krissi realize that the whole process was designed to be permanent. Sure, she might get a massage again someday in the future, but she would never feel the same level of tension that she once had. The mental tension was gone for good. In Krissi's case, as was true for many people who underwent the Mental Relaxation procedure, her brain had been partially rewired to shake off stress, even if that meant it was harder to remain focused. It also tended to wake people up to the sexual needs of their bodies and, in that regard, Krissi was no different. Sex with Blake had become a constant in their relationship and she could not imagine it any other way.

"But I guess it's time to trade in a few brain cells for bigger boobs," Krissi lamented.

"Don't be sad about it," Penny said. "You'll feel tons better when it's all over. Trust me."

Somehow hearing Penny tell her she would feel better about it when it was over helped. And strangely, Krissi did trust Penny. In reality, she had little reason to do so. It was Penny's job to keep the customers happy and to get them to keep spending money. Krissi was already signed up to do that. However, she felt an affinity toward Penny, like they were both on similar journeys. It was the same way with Abbi and Nikki, although Krissi felt like she was always playing catchup with her friends. They were always at least one step ahead of her.

"Thanks, Penny," Krissi said.

"I'll go get Gabby," Penny said as she stood up. Her large breasts bounced and jiggled in her low-cut top. The pink fabric stretched almost to its breaking point to keep her contained. Due to that fact, it had no hope of reaching the top of her skirt, which was a matching pink and only barely fell below the curve of her ass. The whole getup was sexy, but also pretty slutty. Not that Krissi minded. Penny looked good that way and she could wear what she wanted as long as she did not scare off any potential customers. And Krissi was certainly not scared off by the receptionist.

Krissi sat down and picked up a magazine to peruse while she waited. This one seemed much more extreme than the first magazine she had read at Magic Woman. The women in the pictures all had large breasts and come hither looks in their eyes. They were hot and they looked like they were ready to fuck the first guy they came across.

As she sat there, Krissi shifted slightly in her chair, suddenly more aware of her own arousal. She was not as desperate as the women in the magazine appeared to be, but she was counting down the hours until she was scheduled to meet up with Blake. She needed to feel his cock inside of her soon. Of course, she doubted that would be an issue once he saw the new and improved Krissi.

"Penny tells me you're going by Krissi now," Gabby said as she stepped into the reception area.

Krissi looked up to see an almost normal looking Gabby. She was not decked out in club clothes. Her makeup actually looked cute, as opposed to her usual sexy look. That was not to say that Gabby did not look sexy. She oozed with it, as always, but this time in a less in your face way.

"No clubbing last night?" Krissi countered as she dropped the magazine on the table and started to follow Gabby into the back.

"A rare night," Gabby said. "Then again, Wednesdays aren't exactly high on the clubbing list."

Krissi nodded her head. She had moved her appointment to Thursday. Normally she would be at work at this hour, but she was taking a couple days off.

"You still look as good as ever," Krissi commented. "You just look different."

"Thanks," Gabby said. "And you look pretty good yourself now. I like the shoes."

Krissi looked down to the heels on her feet. She had more and more been wearing heels. They had become a staple for whenever she went out with Blake or with the girls. And they had more and more become common when she was at work.

Blake had even bought her a pair of high-heeled slippers she could wear when she stayed over at his house, which was most nights now. It felt like the only time she was ever at her apartment anymore was to drop off her rent check. It seemed a waste to pay all that money for what basically amounted to a storage unit, but she was not yet ready to propose cohabitation, even if they already seemed to have reached that point.

"Thanks," Krissi said, smiling. The white cork-soled wedge sandals had proven to be both fashionable and comfortable, as far as high heels went. Krissi was still adapting to the higher heels, but she never regretted how good they looked. And they gave her butt a little extra boost, so there was no harm in that.

Krissi had completed her outfit with a white pleated tennis skirt and a stretchy pink top. On the recommendation of Penny when she made her appointment, she had foregone wearing a bra or panties. Neither would fit her properly when she was done at Magic Woman.

"So, what brings this on?" Gabby asked as they walked back to her booth. "Usually women have a reason behind taking the next step with the Baby Makeover."

"It's a long story," Krissi answered. "But I think the time is right, you know? My friends did it and they look great and I've never seen them happier. My boyfriend is thrilled, as you might imagine. And I'll be honest. I kind of like the idea of, well, looking hotter. I've already got so much, but there's always room for improvement. And it's not like I'm going to miss being all brainy all the time. I'm switching positions at work to take some of that load off. And then me and my boyfriend are going away for a long weekend to a house on a lake to celebrate. So I guess, it just makes sense, you know?"

"Sounds like a lot of fun, if you ask me," Gabby said. "And

I just know you're gonna love the results. And so is your boyfriend."

Krissi gave a little shiver at the comment about Blake liking her makeover. She was sure he would, but just the thought of him getting hard at the sight of her body was enough to send a spike to her arousal.

Sitting down in the chair, Krissi waited for further instructions from Gabby. Her stylist was busy at the counter, arranging the tools she would need for today's makeover.

"Here's how it's going to work," Gabby said as she pulled out a set of sunglasses. However, the long trailing wire coming off them, as well as the blackout lenses, made it clear these were no ordinary sunglasses. "Most of the procedure you won't be awake for. As you already know, there is a mental component to the Baby Makeover and that is what these glasses are for. They will work on your mental outlook while I focus on your body."

Krissi swallowed hard, her fear spiking as she was reminded that this was the most invasive change she had gone through yet. As much as she was looking forward to the end result, there were still aspects of the whole process that scared her, especially when it came to the mental manipulation. She was already clearly aware that her mind had been manipulated. She may not have understood that when she underwent the Mental Relaxation, but it was clear now. Her mind, her focus, had not been the same since.

Not that Krissi had any complaints about how her mind now worked. She appreciated spending her days worry and anxiety free. But the problem was that it was hard to remain focused on a pressing deadline when she no longer had it in her to worry about it. There had been two incidents since then where Krissi had needed outside help to finish reports on time. And if she was honest with herself, it was those two incidents that led her back to Magic Woman, not to complain, but to take the next step. After all, she had requested the change in her job title and functions.

"Do you want to know the details or would you rather be surprised?" Gabby asked.

Krissi was shocked for a moment. She had never been fully aware of all the improvements Gabby had been set to make before she made them. Being asked was nice. However, as she sat there, Krissi realized she preferred being surprised. She did not want to know how big her boobs would get until she woke up to see them. It was the same with the rest of her. She wanted to be surprised, just like Blake would be surprised when she got home that night.

"Surprise me."

"All right, Krissi," Gabby said as she slid the sunglasses onto Krissi's face. "I'll see you on the other side."

13

W hile Krissi had taken the day off from work, that had not been the case for Blake, even though he was the one planning their long weekend at the lake. It was therefore important that Krissi find the right way to surprise him with her new upgrades when he returned home. The only problem was thinking was no longer considered one of Krissi's strong suits.

It was not that the Baby Makeover at Magic Woman had made Krissi dumb. It was more that it had slowed her mind, making it easier to distract her with shiny or pretty objects. And despite the expensive and impressive house Blake owned and that Krissi almost exclusively lived in, after returning from her makeover, she was certain that the prettiest object in the house was herself. Every time she came to a mirror or caught her reflection in a window, she stopped to gaze at herself, fully in love with everything Gabby had done for her.

First and foremost, Krissi's boobs were everything she could have ever hoped for. They were big without dominating her frame. They were perky too, not needing a bra to hold them up. Not that Krissi had any bras that fit her expanded assets now.

That was also true for Krissi's ass. It now looked like she had spent hours upon hours performing heavy squats to make her butt nice and round. Of course, that was one area where she did not need to worry about her panties fitting her. She largely wore thongs or other types of panties that did not actually cover her butt.

However, those were not the only physical changes that Krissi had noticed. Her lips were more plump. They required more lipstick to keep them properly covered. Not that Krissi minded that. She liked how they looked and she was certain Blake would like the feel of them wrapped around his cock. She could not wait to test them out on his big hard cock.

Somehow Krissi's waist had narrowed even more, further emphasizing her hourglass figure. Or maybe it just looked that way because of her bigger boobs and butt. Either way, Krissi kept lifting her top to get a better look at her taut midriff. She could still see it when she looked down past her boobs, but she had to lean back and crane her neck forward to do it.

However, those actions brought attention to other changes that even Krissi had not expected. She had known about the boobs and the butt and the lips. Those had been expected from what she had seen from Abbi and Nikki when they underwent the same procedure. Gabby changed things up for Krissi, giving her a little hardware to go with her new fleshy assets. Most noticeable was Krissi's new belly-button piercing. She just sported a small gold barbell there now, but with the amazing work done at Magic Woman, the piercing was fully healed and could sport long dangling jewelry whenever she wanted. She just needed to buy some. Or Blake could buy it. He loved showering her with gifts like that.

Krissi had never been one to wear lots of jewelry before

she met Blake. However, he liked buying her jewelry to, as he phrased it, enhance her beauty. She was not going to complain. Even now, she wore a crystal pendant of some sort with a gold chain. It perfectly fell into her cleavage, helping further draw the eye to her improved features.

The belly-button was not the only piercing addition Krissi now sported either. It was one that she did not even realize had been added until she was walking out of Magic Woman and toward her car. Every step she took seemed to give her clit a little ping, turning her on more and more. It was only when she was in the relative safety of her car that Krissi lifted her skirt to discover what had been done. There was a small piece of jewelry pierced through her clit hood that rested directly on her clit. Every step she had taken and caused the ball end to bounce and strike her clit.

Krissi might have been angry about such an addition. Or at least Kristen might have been angry about it. However, the new and improved Krissi was left excited by it. Not only did she find the additional jewelry attractive, she enjoyed the way her increased arousal caused her to wiggle her ass a bit more when she walked. It made her feel even more like a sexual object, always turned on and ready to be used by her boyfriend.

Now that she was back at Blake's house, she not only had to figure out how to best surprise Blake with the new her, she also had to pack for their weekend away. She had plenty of clothes that could fit her, even with her expanded assets, but if she was completely honest with herself, there was only one thing she wanted to wear. Luckily, she had more than enough bikinis to get through the weekend, where she never had to wear the same one for more than a few hours at a time. And that would certainly save on space in her suitcase, leaving more room for shoes.

When Blake arrived home, he walked in the front door

to find Krissi posed on the couch wearing a gold bikini. His cock went instantly hard the moment he saw her with her bigger boobs. He had been aware of what she was doing. It had made his workday more difficult, not just because he needed to prepare to miss a few days of work, but also to be completely incommunicado the whole time. The lake house had a spotty cell signal at best and he wanted to fully devote his time away to relaxing and enjoying himself with Krissi.

"Look at you," Blake said with a wide smile. "You're turning out better than I had ever hoped."

"Thanks, stud," Krissi said with a hungry and horny stare. She licked her lips, feeling every bit the hot and horny girlfriend that she now was. "How do you want to fuck me first?"

"Patience," Blake said as she set down his briefcase and loosened his tie. "I want to get a full look at you first."

Krissi stood up and slowly turned around for her boyfriend, showing him everything. Everything, that is, except for what she had hidden under the thong bottoms of her bikini.

Blake pulled Krissi into him, her ass pushing into his bulging cock. His hands started on her boobs. He squeezed them and pinched them, leaving Krissi a moaning mess as she pushed her ass back against his cock, arching her back and further pushing out her tits into his hands.

"That feels so good," she moaned.

However, Blake was not done exploring his girlfriend's new body. One hand moved up her chest, then light skimmed her neck, making her breath catch in her throat. Finally he reached her lips as he slipped one finger, and then several, into her mouth. Krissi started sucking automatically, treating his fingers as if they were a cock. And in her lust addled mind, she may have thought they were a cock. After all, she needed a cock, and she was willing to take one in any of her holes.

Blake's other hand slipped down across her exposed midriff. His fingers briefly fiddled with the jewelry that now decorated her belly-button, before moving further south. Soon his hand was probing her between her legs, through the fabric of her bikini.

"Oh?" Blake said in surprise. "What's this?"

Krissi shuddered with pleasure as he teased her clit while tracing the outline of the jewelry she now wore between her legs.

"Clit hood piercing," she managed to mumble around Blake's fingers. Not that her words were in any way intelligible when she had three fingers between her lips. But Blake was smart enough to know what his fingers had found, even without understanding Krissi's words.

"No wonder you want to fuck so much," Blake said. "I've heard women get turned on by these. And I bet it's even harder right now because you're not used to it yet."

Krissi nodded her head in agreement.

"Well, I had been hoping for a blowjob," Blake said. "Or even a tit-fuck with your new boobs. But I suppose I can be patient and wait for those. We'll be spending the whole weekend together up at the lake. Fucking you now seems like the humanitarian thing to do."

Krissi nodded her head enthusiastically this time. That was exactly what she wanted. Yes, she would have happily done anything Blake wanted, but what she really wanted was for him to fuck her pussy with that big cock of his. She needed an orgasm desperately.

Before Krissi knew it, she was leaning over the back of the couch. Her bikini bottoms had been pulled away, leaving her pussy bare. She pushed out her ass, positioning herself on her high heels to better take Blake's cock.

"Yes," Krissi moaned, her eyes rolling up into the back of her head, as Blake stuck his cock into her pussy. After that, she was cumming. She could not help herself. She had been so turned on that she was ready to cum as soon as his cock was inside of her. That did not stop Blake from fucking her. After all, he needed his pleasure too. However, by the time Blake was ready to cum, Krissi had already worked her way back up and was ready to cum with him.

Their bodies came together in a symphony of sexual delights. Blake's orgasm felt like an eruption as his cock spilled his seed into Krissi's pussy, filling her up with a day's worth of pent up tension. For Krissi, it felt like an explosion went off inside her, sending a massive shockwave up her spine from her pussy up into her brain. She nearly collapsed, her brain fighting to remain conscious, something it only barely succeeded in.

"Wow," Blake said as he pulled out of Krissi's pussy. "That was unlike anything I have ever experienced before."

"Me too," Krissi agreed, a big dopey smile plastered on her face. Her arms were barely able to hold her up and she continued to lean over the couch, her ass still thrust high in the air. It had been an impromptu coupling, but it was one that she doubted she would ever forget. She had never cum so hard in her life. And to do it twice in one bout made it all the more impressive.

"You can stay that way for a while if you need to," Blake said. "I'm going to go up and shower and then start packing for our drive in the morning. I can't wait to spend a whole weekend in almost complete privacy with you."

Before Blake went upstairs, he took one more look at his sexually satisfied girlfriend. He truly was amazed at these latest changes. She had gone from what he thought was a seven on his list to a ten in just over half a year. And he would have been happy if she had stayed the way she was. But he also had no doubts that this version of Krissi was far superior to her old self. She was a nine or ten now. And after the weekend, he knew they would get to spend even more time together.

"Take your time," Blake reiterated as he slapped Krissi's ass. She let out a giggle followed by a moan. She was still recovering from her double orgasm. And from the sounds she had made, Blake figured it could be anywhere from five to 30 minutes before she was back to moving around again. That would give him time to shower at least.

* * *

It was Saturday afternoon and Krissi was laying out on the front of the boat, just wearing a pair of thong bikini bottoms. She had shucked off the top at some point and not bothered to put it back on. The hot summer sun felt amazing on her already tanned tits. Despite their rapid increase in size, they felt more real than Krissi could remember her old small boobs feeling. It had only been two days with them, but they already felt more a part of her than she had ever considered before.

Sure, there had been a few times when Krissi had forgotten about her new size. Even that morning, she had opened a cabinet in the kitchen and it had slammed almost painfully into her boobs. She was not used to their dimensions, but she was getting very familiar with how good they felt. Their sensitivity was unreal.

That sensitively had been full display the night before when she gave Blake her first tit-fuck. The simple act of using her boobs to get him off was hot enough, but she had almost cum from just the act of fucking him with her boobs. She had needed little help reaching her own climax when

Blake decided to return the favor by fingering her to a nice and strong orgasm.

Blake was fishing off the back of the boat as Krissi sunbathed. She had little interest in fishing. That was something men did. As a woman, her job was to focus on what she did best. And what Krissi did best was look sexy and be the most fuckable girlfriend that she could be. And that meant sitting out in the sun, staying nice and oiled up with sunscreen and other oils.

Not that Krissi needed to worry about tan lines on her boobs or anywhere else. Gabby and the amazing work done at Magic Woman had seen to that. But that did not stop the afternoon sun from feeling amazing on her smooth skin. It was so much easier to just sit back and clear her head than it used to be. She had once been a woman who overthought everything. But that was in the past. Now it was completely normal for Krissi to just shut out all distractions and clear her mind of everything. It was pleasant too. Krissi had never realized how much not thinking felt so good. Had she known, she might have tried it before.

"I caught our dinner," Blake announced as the boat rocked gently, an indication that he had left his perch at the back of the boat and moved forward. "The fish are sitting on ice, so we can stay out here as long as you want."

Krissi opened her eyes and squinted up through her sunglasses. She watched as Blake sat down beside her. He had cleaned himself up. He no longer looked like someone who had been fishing. She certainly could not smell it on him.

"Damn, you're beautiful," Blake said as he reached out and pinched one of Krissi's nipples.

She moaned in response, her arousal rising quickly. Even just laying out on the front of the boat, she had been turned on. Her body always seemed to be thrumming with sexual energy and desire. Even just laying there, she had been wet enough to fuck, had Blake made himself available. That seemed to be her new baseline since her makeover.

And as much as Krissi's thinking had simplified following her trip to Magic Woman, there were a few things she thought about more. Sex was chief among those things. Her first thought about almost any object she saw was about how it could be used during sex, either as a toy or prop, or as a piece of furniture to fuck on or against. A chair or table no longer just held the simple functions they were designed for. Krissi could not help but imagine herself bent over those objects as Blake fucked her from behind. There were even more acrobatic ideas she had, but those would require more than just an impromptu fuck. Those needed planning and communication.

"You know," Blake said as he sat there admiring his girl-friend's boobs. "You don't need those bottoms."

Krissi giggled, but said nothing as he started pulling gently at the tie sides of her bikini bottoms. She let him have his way with her. That just added to the fun.

"And you know what else?" Blake said. "I haven't seen anyone around all day, so I think we can have some fun out here on the boat."

Krissi giggled some more, but this time she was excited. She knew exactly what kind of fun Blake was talking about and she was all in. She could never say no to sex with him.

14

It had been a magical weekend at the lake. Krissi had been fucked more times than she could count and she had never worn more than a bikini the entire trip. When they drove back Sunday afternoon, they had stopped at a local diner for a quick bite to eat. The only change Krissi had made from her bikini wearing was that she added a sheer sarong to add a little more cover. Not that it did anything to hide her body. It was just the bare minimum that would allow her entrance.

Not that anyone at the diner that afternoon, primarily a group of fishermen who were on their way home from a morning spent doing what they did best before they returned to their day jobs, minded how Krissi was dressed. They all stared. She loved the attention.

That was something else that had changed with her most recent trip to Magic Woman. Krissi was now a glutton for attention. She wanted as many eyes on her as possible. It was the best way to reassure herself that she was indeed a hot piece of ass, a sexual object to be desired by men and women alike. After all, why else would she only bring bikinis to wear on the lake trip?

However, despite Krissi's desire to be looked upon as a subject of desire, she only had eyes for Blake. Her boyfriend was more and more becoming her everything. And that was now including her boss.

When Krissi arrived at work on Monday morning, she did so having spent the night at her own apartment. It was her first day in her new role and she did not want anyone to think that she had gotten the job just because her new boss was the same man she was sleeping with. Not that anyone around her believed she was not already fucking him. They all knew. And it was not like she was getting favorable treatment with her change in positions. Actually, her new job paid less.

"Personal assistant to the Vice President of Finance and Accounting," Krissi said to herself as she rode up in the elevator. She had nearly pushed the button for her old floor out of habit. Her cubicle was now empty. Or at least it was empty of her few belongings she had taken with her before taking off for her long weekend. For all she knew, the cubicle had been given to someone else by now. It did not matter. It was no longer her workspace. She now worked on the top floor.

Executive management was divided up into two areas of the top floor of the building. The CEO and other C-level executives worked on the far side of the building. The Vice Presidents all worked on the near side of the building around a common secretarial space. It was in this space that Krissi would be working, alongside Abbi and Nikki. She had finally made the move to join them and, despite the pay cut, she was excited for it.

"Krissi," Nikki squealed as the elevator door opened.

"Let's see them," Abbi added with equal excitement.

Krissi automatically knew what her two friends were talking about as she stepped off the elevator, carrying a box that blocked their view.

Walking expertly across the room in her high heels, she set the box down on what was her new desk. She knew it was hers because it was situated directly in front of Blake's office. It was also the only empty desk available.

"Here you go," Krissi finally said as she opened her coat toward her friends.

Their eyes opened wide in surprise. Krissi had spent a few hours at the mall the night before, after she and Blake had returned to town from their weekend getaway. That had given her the opportunity to buy a few new bras that would fit her expanded assets. She also bought a new outfit for her first day of work. She knew what kind of look she was going for and she wanted to impress on her first day in her new job.

Underneath Krissi's coat—which she had not needed to wear given the summer warmth, but had done so to provide the best reveal she could imagine—she wore a fitted white blouse with as many buttons left undone as she could get away with. Her new purple push-up bra kept wanting to peak out. She had paired the white blouse with a short black skirt. Her stockings failed to reach the hem of her skirt, but the garter straps slipped up underneath to help hold them up. The whole image was definitely the epitome of a sexy secretary.

And for the most part, that was what Krissi now was. Yes, her title was officially a personal assistant, however, that was mostly so Blake could arrange to bring her along on his work trips. As long as she got her work done, they could also fuck whenever he wanted. In Krissi's mind, this was now even more of a plus, considering how much she needed him.

"You look even bigger than us now," Nikki finally said, commenting on Krissi's boobs for the first time.

Krissi giggled, loving the attention and the compliment. Of course, her looking bigger was partly a factor of her boobs getting pushed up by her bra, but she did believe she might have been a little bigger than her friends. And that was something she loved to think about. Up until her most recent trip to Magic Woman, both Abbi and Nikki had always been more beautiful than her. At the very least, they had always been more fashionable and sexy than her. But now she was finally operating on even footing with them and in some areas, like her boobs, she was actually ahead.

Not that it was a serious competition. All three women loved each other and never fought. It was more that they were supportive of each other and always comparing themselves, trying to get the most out of themselves. The difference now was that instead of it being Krissi tagging along with her sexier friends, they were all sexy in their own right. And if anything, with Krissi sporting long blonde hair and having slightly bigger boobs, she was the sexier one by many standards.

"I bet you're glad you got them done," Abbi said. "Doesn't it feel great."

"Oh yeah," Krissi agreed as she shrugged off her coat and hung it up in the corner on the coat rack. She would not need to wear that for the rest of the day. And even when she went home that night, to Blake's house instead of her apartment, she would simply sling it over her arm. It would be too warm to wear it. "I love it. And I especially love what Gabby did for me."

Abbi and Nikki simply watched as Krissi first pulled her blouse free from her skirt and lifted it to show off her new belly-button piercing. "I also have one in my clit hood, but I'll have to show that to you later."

The truth was, Krissi had no qualms with lifting her skirt right there if she needed to. She certainly would have if Blake ordered her to do it. However, she also knew this was her first day and there were random people who could walk in. The elevators were right there and they could open at any moment. The last thing she needed was for the CEO to step off the elevator as she was flashing her pussy and her new jewelry to her friends. Krissi's inhibitions might have been decreased, but her understanding of what was appropriate at various times had not changed. Her actions not only reflected on herself, but on Blake too.

"That's hot," Nikki said as she started to get lost in a fantasy. She tended to do that a lot. Between the three of them, she was the dimmest of them and the most easily distractible. But considering they were all now somewhere on the bimbo spectrum, they were all easily distractible.

"I better get started on my new job," Krissi said. "Blake will be here any moment and he told me he wants to start his day at the office with a protein shake."

Krissi waved to her friends before she shuffled off into her new boss' office to start her work. Blake was spending his early morning playing basketball at his gym. He was going to want a protein shake to help him recover when he arrived. Krissi wanted to make sure everything was perfect for him as soon as he walked in the door.

Just as Krissi had finished making his protein recovery shake, Blake came bouncing through the door to his office.

"How's my new personal assistant doing today?" he asked as he tossed his gym bag into the closet.

Blake approached Krissi with hungry eyes. He wrapped her up in a tight embrace as he took all of her in.

"Yes, I think you'll do nicely," Blake said. Krissi simply giggled her response. "And you even have my protein shake ready. Nice work."

"Thank you, sir," Krissi said as she stepped out of his way as he sat down at his desk.

"Sir. I like that. Maybe that should be how you always refer to me. And I mean both here and at home."

Krissi swallowed hard. This was the first time something work related would go home with them. Then again, they had brought their personal lives to the office enough that the line between the two aspects of their lives was already blurred.

"Anything you want, Sir," Krissi said, this time putting added emphasis on the Sir. And if she was honest with herself, it felt good. It felt right.

"Anything?" Blake said with a raised eyebrow. "Well, what I want right now is a blowjob. Can you do that?"

"Yes, Sir," Krissi said as she jumped into action. A moment later she was under the desk and sucking happily on Blake's cock.

Yes, her new position might have come with a pay cut, but it made her happy in so many ways. It was all worth it.

15

Krissi stood in front of Magic Woman. She took a deep breath and then looked down. She reached up and shifted her boobs in her fuzzy pink sweater, maximizing the cleavage on display. Her hands seemed to rarely be far from her boobs these days. She was always trying to make them look as good as possible. Her sweater was designed to maximize the amount of her boobs she showed off. There was a small clasp just below her boobs to keep the sweater together, turning the whole thing more into a bra with long sleeves than a top. A small band of skin was visible beneath her sweater before her high-waisted skirt started.

The skirt had actually been a tube dress once, before her last trip to Magic Woman. Now, between the strain that her boobs and butt put it under, it was too small. She could either cover her boobs or her butt, but not both. Luckily, by wearing it like this, with a sweater to compliment it, Krissi could still use it. And by keeping more of her skin covered, she could fight off the chilly fall air.

Part of maximizing her cleavage was just Krissi's desire to always look her best. The rest could easily be explained by the recent visits to Magic Woman by Abbi and Nikki. They had finally decided to go all the way and get the Full Makeover. Their tits were big and their brains small. They were perfect little bimbos now.

There was no question about what Krissi was about to do. She had already discussed it with Blake. He had been the perfect gentleman, making it clear that she did not have to do this for him, but that he would support her if she chose to. That support, coupled with Abbi and Nikki pushing her to join them, Krissi had made her appointment.

However, the timing of her visit to Magic Woman was crucial in Krissi's mind. She and Blake were headed to Hawaii for a week. It was the perfect fall vacation getaway. What was more, Krissi had the suspicion that Blake was set to propose to her. She already knew her answer and she wanted the engagement photos to look amazing. And she knew, without a doubt, that she would look like the perfect bride-to-be after a trip to her favorite salon and spa. Magic Woman had made her the woman she now was and she knew she had so much more to do.

"Krissi," Penny squealed when Krissi finally walked inside. "I thought you'd never come in. Having second thoughts?"

"Nope," Krissi said with a giggle. "I just wanted to make my boobs look better."

That got Penny to giggle too.

"I think my boyfriend is going to propose next week, so I want to look my best," Krissi added.

"Oh, totally," Penny said. "I get that. And I'm sure you'll look great when Gabby gets done with you. Make yourself comfortable while I go get Gabby for you."

Krissi sat down and immediately started thumbing through a magazine. She did not bother to read any of the words. She rarely read at all anymore. She needed to for work, but even then she kept it to a minimum. Even her abilities with numbers were beginning to fade. She could still remember them, a helpful skill while working for the Vice President of Finance and Accounting, but the mental number manipulation skills she once had had atrophied. Even simple math usually required a calculator now.

Not that Krissi missed those things in the slightest. She had more important things to think about, like how to best take care of her man. Even at work, that was her number one priority. She no longer thought about their relationship having a sex life. Their sex was so frequent, it was simply a part of her relationship. There was no way to separate it away, especially given how frequently Blake's cock was somewhere inside her at work. The extra eight hours spent together every day made it seem like the frequency of sex had doubled. Not that Krissi was complaining. She was a horny girl and needed it as much as Blake did.

"How would you like me this morning, Sir?" she would ask when Blake came into the office. He often had dropped her off on the way to the gym. She could get started on her day while he worked out. When he arrived at the office, she had everything ready for him. And she made it a point to make herself fully accessible. Krissi had even started keeping a tube of lube in her desk, just in case Blake wanted to fuck her ass. It was a rarity, but he had his moments. She never had imagined that would be a part of her sex repertoire, but she had learned to enjoy it. She could even cum from it.

Of course, calling Blake Sir was caught on completely. It was the only name she used for him. The only time she ever used his real name was when she absolutely needed to, like when talking to family about her boyfriend. Even among her friends, which were almost exclusively Abbi and Nikki now, she simply called him Sir. They each had their own names for their boyfriends, so it was no big deal.

Looking at the pictures in the magazine, Krissi could enjoy how hot many of the women looked. However, she could also see that they all had room for improvement. In many ways, she was already sexier than many of the women she saw. That would become even more true once she finished her appointment. She would be a hot and sexy bimbo from now on and she was going to love every moment of it.

"Krissi," Gabby called out when she entered the reception area. "I'm ready for you."

Krissi looked up to see a new and improved Gabby. She still looked like she had been out clubbing the night before, but now she looked like a proper babe with big tits.

"I like the tits," Krissi said as she put the magazine down and pushed herself up so she was standing in her high heels. Even without the help from Magic Woman, her tendons had shortened, making it necessary to always wear some kind of higher heel. Even her trainers had a raised heel in them.

Gabby laughed as she grabbed her tits, almost like she was presenting them to Krissi. "Thanks. I got them last month. I've never been more popular at the clubs."

"I bet," Krissi said, licking her lips. "Maybe you could give me a set like that."

"I might just do that," Gabby said with a wink. "Now come on back and let's turn you into your perfect bimbo self."

When Krissi first started coming to Magic Woman, the word bimbo had never been mentioned. However, it was clear as day that each package the salon and spa offered was designed to take the client down the path toward bimbodom. And now that Krissi was an active participant in her own bimbofication, choosing to complete her transformation, it could be talked about openly. Krissi was already on the bimbo spectrum. She could be considered a baby bimbo, a good description after undergoing the Baby Makeover. However, now she was going all the way, undergoing the Full Makeover to make her a full bimbo. She could not wait.

Krissi followed Gabby back to the now familiar booth. As she sat down, she took a moment to unhook the clasp at the front of her sweater, letting her boobs breathe freely. She also rolled up her skirt around her waist, giving Gabby full access.

"I asked last time and I'll ask again," Gabby said once Krissi was settled. "Do you want the details or do you want to be surprised?"

"Surprise me," Krissi said with a giggle. "I just want to wake up as a bimbo."

"This should be fun," Gabby said as she slid the now familiar glasses onto Krissi's face.

As soon as the lights started to dance in front of Krissi's eyes, she felt herself sinking deeper and deeper, her mind going more and more blank. She fully realized that this was going to be the end of her life as a career woman. There would be no going back to her old accounting job, assuming she wanted that. No, Krissi had given up on everything that had once defined her old self. It was all about being the perfect bimbo for Blake. She just wanted to be his pretty plaything. And it was a desire that was about to come true.

16

K rissi watched with teary eyes as Blake got down on one knee.

The pair were in Hawaii for a week-long vacation. For Krissi, it had been more than a non-stop sex-fest with her boyfriend. It had also been both a debut and a chance to better understand her new body and mind.

When Krissi had left Magic Woman, she had been unable to wipe the smile off her face. Her sweater barely fit over her now big tits. She was certain she had once again moved to the top of the secretarial pool when it came to the size of her tits. Abbi and Nikki were very close seconds. However, Gabby still ended up being a bit bigger, but she had always been bigger than Krissi, so there was little surprise that her body was not quite ready to go that big yet.

Not that a return to Magic Woman for another size increase was out of the question. Such things were possible, but it would all be up to Blake.

Despite Krissi's devotion to Blake before her Full Makeover, she still had the potential to be an independent woman. She could have broken things off with the man she called Sir. She would have likely found herself in the arms of another wealthy and handsome man in short order, but she was not fully dependent on him.

That had now changed. Krissi was in some ways, a hollow shell of her old self. The woman who had once been known as Kristen was simply no more. She had fully embraced being a bimbo, leaving decisions beyond what clothes to wear up to the man she loved with all her heart. All Krissi now wanted to do was please him, using her body to fullest effect.

And it was a body that Blake found beyond pleasing. Her tits were big, yes. They no longer needed a bra either. Not that Krissi would forgo wearing them completely. They had their purposes to help her look sexy.

Additionally, her ass had been rounded out even more. There would always be a question whether she had work done there or if she was naturally susceptible to the effects of squats and other similar gym exercises.

Krissi's lips had also gotten another boost. Now there was no question what they were best suited for. They were dick sucking lips. Of course, Krissi's blowjob skills were aided by more than just the size of her lips. Her gag reflex had been removed entirely. She could deepthroat any cock that presented itself to her. Then there was the tongue piercing. The bright pink barbell piercing her tongue had been a popular addition and Krissi took great pride in having her head shoved onto Blake's cock regularly.

There were other changes too, more subtle than those already mentioned. Krissi's eyelashes had been lengthened. They helped draw more attention to how her eyes now only seemed to show lust. There was no intelligence remaining for her to display.

Not that Krissi would be useless in her job. She would

still be able to remember a few facts and figures, important items to impress Blake and the important people he held meetings with. She would still be able to operate the phones and the computers. She would just be a lot slower. Her typing had devolved from reasonably efficient coordination to a hunt and peck method that was slow, but highlighted her now longer nails.

Essentially, if Krissi had been at worst a nine after the Baby Makeover, now the dial had been turned up to 11. Blake did not even realize the scale went that high. But when it came to Krissi, she had always overachieved in his eyes. She had worked hard in her old accounting role. Too hard, in his eyes, but it was an effort he appreciated. Now she had turned all that effort toward herself and their relationship. Krissi might never be seen as an accountant again, but he had no doubt she would be happy. After all, it was his responsibility to make her happy. And it was a responsibility he did not take lightly.

"Krissi," Blake said as he pulled out the ring. "Will you marry me?"

She already knew her answer before he asked. She had anticipated this moment coming before she had turned herself into a bimbo. But that knowledge did little to prevent the tsunami of emotion to inundate her, making it hard to think, let alone speak.

Finally Krissi nodded her head. "Yes, Sir," she squeaked out.

Her voice even caught Blake off guard. It had been raised at least an octave. She could not help but sound girlish when she spoke, but that only seemed to fit with her hyper-feminine bimbo style. And despite her always having been a bit of a screamer during sex, it had quieted the noise a little, making it easier to fuck her in semi-public places.

Blake took the time to properly place the ring on Krissi's finger. It was a perfect fit. He had bought her enough jewelry over the past few months to know her ring size. And the large diamond rock on the ring was both a signal of Blake's incredible wealth, but also of his devotion to his now fiancée. He wanted nothing more than for her to always turn heads as his trophy wife. It was a role she had designed herself for, whether she had understood her undertaking at the beginning or not. And Blake had every intention of making sure she never regretted anything, whether she still could or not.

Krissi was thankful the pictures came later. She had time to fix her face after shedding tears of joy. She could not stand the idea of being photographed without looking her best. Given what was left of her mind, her appearance was all she had left. And she was thankful that Blake was happy to have a sexy bimbo as his wife and not some brainiac rocket scientist or financial whiz.

And those pictures, when finally released to friends and family, showed Krissi's true self. They showed her complete joy in becoming engaged to the man she viewed as the best man in the world. He was not just wealthy and handsome. He was kind and caring. He was everything she had ever wanted in a partner and so much more. And she was thankful for every moment they would get to spend together.

"How about we take some of our own pictures?" Blake offered after the engagement photographer left. His arms were still wrapped around Krissi's waist as he pulled her back against his body. They gazed out at the ocean together, enjoying the closeness they had finally made official.

Krissi had her hands wrapped around Blake's hands. Her ring was on full display. It was the signal that she now belonged to him. Yes, stupid men would still hit on her, which was not unappreciated, but the smart ones would know what she was taken, that she was now owned. And she considered herself lucky to be owned by such a man as Blake.

"Ooh, you naughty man," Krissi said. "I would love to, Sir."

Krissi craned her neck upward and to the side, kissing Blake with her plump lips, her pierced tongue darting into his mouth. She could never say no to him. And she never wanted to say no to him either.

17

When Krissi had last attended the annual company New Year's Eve party, she had felt depressed about the whole thing. She had been underdressed and had found herself counting down the minutes until she could leave. As far as she was concerned, her appearance there had been a complete disaster.

But that had been when she was Kristen. She had been a recent hire in the accounting department. And that was when she had been overwhelmed by unfamiliar social interactions. So much had changed since then.

When Krissi stepped into the party, holding tightly to Blake's arm, she looked completely different. Her body had undergone a complete metamorphosis. Gone was the short dirty blonde hair. Gone too was her pale skin and flat body. In its place was a body of bimbo perfection, with big tits, a nice round ass, and a long mane of wavy platinum blonde hair.

Krissi was also no longer the shy fly on the wall that she had been a year earlier. She was vivacious, happy to talk to anyone, as long as they did not want to talk about anything complicated. And if they did, she was perfectly happy to just giggle her way through the conversation. The important part was being present and actually having the conversation.

Another big change was how Krissi was dressed. Her outfit from the year before had been a blue sweater and black slacks. Krissi could no longer understand how she could have worn such an outfit. She had not even been wearing high heels to the party. Compared to a year ago, Krissi's style had completely changed. She still wore sweaters, but only in ways that highlighted her body, especially her tits. And the only time she wore pants was when they were of the tight leather variety. And Krissi could not remember the last time her heels naturally touched the ground. She lived in high heels completely.

A year ago, she had spent a lot of time psyching herself up to attend the party, needing to collect as much mental energy as she could to make it through. This year, that time was spent making sure she looked her absolute best in her special gown. The outfit was definitely a bit gaudy, but such things were more acceptable when coming from a known bimbo. And there were few doubts at the company that Krissi was a bimbo. She looked like one and she acted like one. The fact she did her job well was the only reason people were not critical of her. It was no secret that she was engaged to her boss.

However, more than anything, more than her fantastic body or her being perched on Blake's arm all night, the thing that everyone would remember about her this year was her gown. The sheer gown that was pulled tight around her every curve was covered in small pieces of mirrored glass, fitting the New Year's Eve theme perfectly. She was her own dropping ball, her dress casting off reflected light like a disco ball.

Not that every inch of Krissi was covered in such material. Her tits were still well highlighted with a deep valley of cleavage on full display. So too was a good deal of her legs. It would not take much to discover that she was not wearing any panties.

"Abbi, Nikki," Krissi squealed when she saw her two best friends. The three bimbos embraced each other with hugs and kisses. They were perfectly happy to mash their big tits together in an attractive display of girl-on-girl affection. It got even more heated when they turned to open mouth kissing. Their men certainly did not mind them being so loving toward each other. In fact, letting them blow off a little sexual energy with each other from time to time saved the men the hassle of always being ready to fuck them.

"Your dress is so fucking sexy," Nikki said enthusiastically. "I'm jelly."

"Your dress is sexy too," Krissi countered.

And it was. Nikki was dressed in a red backless dress with a cowl neck that reached her belly-button. Her bulbous ass was barely contained in the tight stretchy material of her dress and her legs were well displayed from the slit up the side. And that slit went high enough that it was pretty clear Nikki was not wearing panties either.

"Ah, thanks," Nikki said. "You're, like, the bestest. You both are."

"I don't know what I'd do without you two," Krissi said. "Last year I didn't feel like I belonged, but I don't feel that way anymore. You two helped me fit in as a proper sexy bimbo."

"I'm glad you came around," Abbi said. "I was worried about you when we first introduced ourselves."

"I bet you don't worry anymore," Krissi teased.

"Only if I'm sexy enough for Darren," Abbi answered.

"You're definitely sexy," Nikki said.

"Especially wearing that dress," Krissi added.

Abbi's gown was green to match her eyes and to contrast with her red hair. It looked a bit like a Playboy Bunny outfit, the way it hugged her body, but with a sheer skirt that did nothing to hide her legs. Her dress would make it a bit more difficult to get in or out of, but it looked good, especially as it attempted to contain her round ass. It failed, but that only made it better.

"Thanks, girls," Abbi said.

As the three bimbos chatted, their men wandered off together. After all, not only were the three women the best of friends, but their men were good friends as well. And the three bimbos could be counted on not to get into too much trouble if left alone for a few minutes. They were still functioning adults, barely. They just had very different ideas of how to behave than the majority of people.

Not that the three bimbos stood out that much. This was very much a high end party. All the men wore tuxedos and the women wore gowns. The only difference was how sexy and at times revealing their three gowns could be. And attention getting, especially with Krissi there. No one could stop from giving her at least a once over before moving on. She was the brightest person in the room, in a literal sense only.

The party was great fun. Krissi even managed to drag Blake away for a few minutes so he could fuck her in one of the upstairs bedrooms of the host house. She had been on edge since she had sucked Blake's cock on the ride to the party. There had not been time for her to cum too. He had her suck on a dildo she kept in her purse to prevent her from screaming out too loud. Not that there was much reason to keep quiet. Between the din of the party downstairs and the squeals and screams of Abbi and Nikki getting railed by their boyfriends in other rooms, it was unlikely Krissi would be heard.

The whole night had been a huge success and the countdown to midnight had made it all worth it. As the clock struck midnight, Blake kissed his fiancée hard on the lips as he generously grabbed one of her tits through her dress. Krissi reveled in the moment, loving being a bimbo plaything for Blake.

Afterward, when the party was finally starting to break up and Blake was leading Krissi toward the door, the bimbo spotted a familiar sight. Standing off in the corner, not sure what to do with herself, was a woman that reminded Krissi of the woman she used to be. She wore a white frumpy sweater and an ankle length black skirt with black trainers on her feet. That was no way to dress for a fun New Year's Eve party, but Krissi knew how to help.

"Excuse me, Sir," Krissi said. "I need to talk to someone real quick and stuff."

Krissi broke away from her fiancé and approached the woman. She still wore her shiny gown, but she had added a white bolero jacket to cover her shoulders and arms. It did little more than that. Even if it had been designed to close, there was no way it could have closed around her prodigious chest.

"Hi there," Krissi said.

"Um, hello," the woman said hesitantly. She had not been expecting to be noticed by anyone, especially by someone like Krissi.

"I'm Krissi."

"I know. They hired me as your replacement in accounting. I, um, don't understand what happened to you, but you were a good accountant before."

Krissi giggled. "Thanks, but I don't do that stuff anymore."

"I gathered. Oh, I'm Rebecca."

"It's nice to meet you," Krissi said with a genuine smile.

"Um, but why come talk to me?" Rebecca looked down at

the ring on Krissi's finger and then up at Blake who stood by the door, waiting for her. "It looks like your fiancé is waiting for you."

"I wanted to give you this," Krissi said as she reached into her purse and pulled out a card. The words Magic Woman were printed in large lettering on one side. "The folks there helped me a lot last year to help me fit in better. I was under-dressed and out of my league at the last party. The people there helped me. I bet they can help you too."

"Oh, um, well, thanks," Rebecca said.

"Just call the number and give Penny the code on the back of the card. You won't regret it."

Before Rebecca could say anything more, Krissi turned and rejoined her fiancé. Just before they walked through the door and out into the cold, Krissi turned one last time and waved. She vaguely wondered if next year the trio of bimbos would be a foursome. Rebecca would make a great Bekki. And maybe the new Vice President in charge of Manufac-turing needed a girlfriend. Rebecca had potential. Krissi might need to fan the flames a bit when they returned to work next week. After all, it was so much easier to fit in as a bimbo.

ABOUT THE AUTHOR

Sadie Thatcher is a longtime author of erotic fiction, especially related to transformations and bimbofication. She likes to say "I have thrown off the shackles of my conservative upbringing and now write erotic stories."

She maintains several blogs devoted to her writings, including a behind the scenes look at her writing process, and bimbos in general, as well as highlights works by other authors. They can be found at:

https://authorsadiethatcher.tumblr.com
https://buildingbettergiggles.tumblr.com

Acting the Part

Subliminal Society

Inheritance

Company Morale

His Bimbo Girlfriend

The Bimbo Room

The Bimbos of Blossom

Dr. Jekyll and Missy Hyde

Second Chance

From M&As To T&A

Trading Places

The Bimbo Nutcracker Suite

Milked and Herded

The Curse of Playing Bimbo Tag

The Curse of Playing Bimbo Tag: Jenna or Jenni

The Bimbo Professor: The Curse of Playing Bimbo Tag Book 3

Anything for the Job

Anything for the Job 2

Anything for His Job

The Bimbo in the Mirror

The Bimbo in the Mirror 2

Astrid and the Bimbo Bee

Bella and the Bimbo Bee

Cali and the Bimbo Bee

Desiree and the Bimbo Bee

Ember and the Bimbo Bee

Fiona and the Bimbo Bee

Bimbo Halloween

Bimbo Christmas

Bimbo Technology

Dorm Room Bimbo

Carissa's Magic Pen

Spirit Walk

Muscle Memory

The Case of the Bimbo Wife

Changes

Changes 2

New Year New You

The Bimbo Dream

The Wedding Gift

The Cure

Backfire

Bim & Bo Yoga

Wishing for Each Other

Bimbo Roots

A Bimbo at Oktoberfest

The Lost Bet

The Fountain

Bimbo Ghost

Sugar and Spice and Everything Nice

Basic Bimbo

A Helping Hand

Bimbos in Space

Christmas Train to Bimboton

Letters to Bimbo Claus

Gone Fishing

Body Swap Rings: Happy Anniversary

Body Swap Rings 2: Wedding Night

The Bimbo Experience

The Bimbo Experience 2

The Bimbo Experience 3some

The 4th Bimbo Experience

Bimbo Genes

Bimbo Genes II: The Virus

The Bimbo Genes III: The Epidemic

Bimbo Juice: Blue Raspberry

Bimbo Juice: Grape

Bimbo Juice: Mango

Bimbo Juice: Pineapple

Bimbo Juice: Red Apple

Bimbo Juice: Veggie

Bimbo Juice Gone Wild: The Muse

Bimbo Juice Gone Wild: Street Racer

Bimbo Juice Gone Wild: Score

Bimbos of the Traveling Earrings: Book 1

Bimbos of the Traveling Earrings: Book 2

Bimbos of the Traveling Earrings: Book 3

Bimbos of the Traveling Earrings: Book 4

Bimbo Party: Kennedy

Bimbo Party: Esme

Bimbo Party: Ariana

Bimbo Party: Tara

Workout Buddies

Wishful Thinking

Wanting More

Bimbo Harem: Annabelle

Bimbo Harem: Josie

Bimbo Harem: Nikki

Bimbo Harem: Tiana

Giggle Dust

Giggle Dust 2.0

Giggle Dust 3.0

Giggle Dust 4.0

Bimbo Takeover: The First Step

Bimbo Takeover: Teammates

Bimbo Takeover: Going to the Top

Bimbo Takeover: Revenge of the Bimbos

www.ingramcontent.com/pod-product-compliance
Lightning Source LLC
Chambersburg PA
CBHW072055150726
47999CB00005B/1783